The Secret
of the Forgotten Cave

As she took a sharp turn, Nancy looked in the rearview mirror. She saw the dark outline of a car behind them with its headlights off. "Look, there it is!" she cried.

"You're right!" Bess exclaimed.

Nancy slowed down even further. The car caught up and tailgated them, the front end not more than a couple of inches away from her rear bumper. Why would the driver follow so closely? And how could someone drive so expertly without headlights?

"Nancy, watch out!" Bess cried.

The dark car hit the rear bumper and pushed Nancy's car far to the right. Nancy tried to keep on the road, but it was impossible. Her car hit the wooden rail of the bridge and plowed over the edge, heading straight for the water.

Nancy Drew
Mystery Stories

Available from MINSTREL Books

NANCY DREW® 134

THE SECRET OF THE FORGOTTEN CAVE

CAROLYN KEENE

A MINSTREL® BOOK

Published by POCKET BOOKS

New York   London   Toronto   Sydney   Tokyo   Singapore

A MINSTREL PAPERBACK *Original*

A Minstrel Book published by
POCKET BOOKS, a division of Simon & Schuster Inc.
1230 Avenue of the Americas, New York, NY 10020

Copyright © 1996 by Simon & Schuster Inc.
Produced by Mega-Books, Inc.

ISBN: 0-671-50516-5

First Minstrel Books printing December 1996

10 9 8 7 6 5 4 3 2

Cover art by Ernie Norcia

Printed in the U.S.A.

Contents

THE SECRET OF THE
FORGOTTEN CAVE

1

Aunt Elizabeth's Award

"George, I'm so glad you persuaded us to come to Connecticut with you," Nancy Drew said. She slid out from behind the steering wheel of the car they'd rented at the train station. "What a pretty town Fairport is!"

George Fayne smiled. She closed the car door and joined her slim, golden-haired friend on the sidewalk. "It's like a postcard picture, isn't it?" she said.

George looked into the backseat of the car and saw her cousin, Bess Marvin, struggling with the clasp of her backpack. "Hurry up, Bess," George called.

"Sorry," Bess apologized as she clambered out. "I was looking for my camera, but I guess I must have packed it in my suitcase."

The town green of Fairport stretched out before them. The square took up several blocks and was anchored at one end by a white spired church and at the other by a gazebo, festive with crepe paper decorations fluttering in the spring breeze. In between lay an expanse of clipped grass and tall, stately trees.

Frowning, George ran a hand through her short, dark hair and scanned the crowd gathering around the gazebo. "Aunt Elizabeth told me she'd meet us before the ceremony, but I don't see her."

"Why don't we follow the crowd?" Nancy suggested. "After all, they're here for the same reason we are—to see your aunt."

George's aunt, Elizabeth Porter, was her great-aunt on her father's side of the family. The people of Fairport had gathered to give her an award for her lifelong efforts as a conservationist. Since George's parents hadn't been able to attend, George had asked Nancy and Bess to join her instead, offering a week's vacation at her aunt's colonial home as an added enticement. The two friends had eagerly accepted the invitation.

"Is that her?" Bess asked. She pushed a strand of blond hair behind her ears and placed her other hand above her eyes to shade them from the bright spring sun. She pointed to a gray-haired woman standing in the middle of a circle of people.

"That's her," George replied, walking faster. Nancy and Bess hurried after her.

"Aunt Elizabeth!" George called.

Elizabeth Porter turned when she heard her name, and her face broke into a wide smile. "George! I'm so glad you're here."

George gave her aunt a big hug. "These are my friends," she said, introducing Nancy and Bess.

Elizabeth Porter shook their hands. "I've heard so much about you both," she said, her blue eyes twinkling, "and all your adventures. I hear you're quite the detective, Nancy."

"I've solved a few mysteries," Nancy replied, smiling modestly.

"Well, there's nothing mysterious going on here," Elizabeth Porter said, laughing. "Just an old lady getting a plaque."

Nancy knew right away that she was going to enjoy getting to know George's aunt. Elizabeth Porter was a spirited woman who clearly wasn't afraid to make a joke at her own expense.

According to George, her aunt was an avid gardener who had spent many years launching and organizing beautification projects around the town. She was also a strong-willed woman who had definite opinions about almost everything, but who was also admired for her ability to get things done.

"Mrs. Porter?" A young man came up to

George's aunt and took her elbow. "Are you ready?"

"As ready as I'll ever be," Mrs. Porter replied jauntily. She let herself be led to the gazebo and climbed the stairs to the platform.

Nancy, Bess, and George stepped back into the crowd and waited for the ceremony to begin.

"Well, she's gotten herself involved in another controversy," Nancy heard someone behind her mutter. Without turning, she continued to listen.

"And for bats, of all things!" another voice replied.

Were they referring to Aunt Elizabeth? Nancy wondered. And what kind of bats? The ones that flew or the ones you hit a ball with? What could they possibly mean?

Before she could hear any more of the conversation, the band behind Aunt Elizabeth struck up a rousing tune, signaling the start of the ceremony.

"There's John Stryker, the town manager," George said to Nancy with a nudge of her elbow. Pointing to a distinguished-looking man in a business suit stepping up to the microphone, George added, "He's the bane of Aunt Elizabeth's existence."

"How so?" Nancy asked.

"He's always trying to kill her projects by telling her the town doesn't have the money,"

George replied. "But Aunt E. just holds a fund-raiser and gets around him."

"Shhh!" Bess whispered. "I want to hear!"

John Stryker took the microphone and gave a long-winded speech praising Mrs. Porter for her hard work and determination. Then he shook her hand and gave her an engraved plaque along with an enormous smile.

George gave Nancy a knowing look and rolled her eyes. "Politics," she whispered with a sigh.

Now it was Aunt Elizabeth's turn to speak. Her speech was short and to the point and ended with a joke about how her work had never felt hard—because it had always been exactly what she wanted to do.

The crowd applauded appreciatively.

Nancy was about to whisper to George what she'd overheard the two people behind her say, but the band began to play again. Aunt Elizabeth graciously accepted a bouquet of flowers from a little boy and was then escorted down the gazebo stairs and into a crowd of well-wishers.

Nancy watched as the townspeople of Fairport clustered around Aunt Elizabeth, laughing and hugging her exuberantly. But before George could join her aunt, Nancy pulled her to one side and told her what she'd overheard.

George frowned. "I can't imagine what that's about," she said. "Aunt Elizabeth has a habit of

5

getting people riled up, but in the end she always wins them over to her side."

Bess interrupted. "Look," she said, pointing to a little girl carrying an ice-cream cone. "Do you think that's part of the celebration?"

Nancy nudged George and the two laughed. Bess had a serious sweet tooth.

"I think I'll follow that cone," Bess said, heading after the little girl. "I'll find you two later!"

The crowd around Aunt Elizabeth thinned out enough for Nancy and George to approach her and add their own congratulations. Aunt Elizabeth's face shone with happiness.

"Aunt E., what's this I hear about you and some bats?" George finally asked when the last well-wisher had left.

The smile abruptly disappeared from Aunt Elizabeth's face. "How did you hear about that?"

"I overheard someone in the crowd saying something about it," Nancy explained.

"Well," Aunt Elizabeth said, "we've got a bit of a predicament here in Fairport. And I'm afraid I'm in the middle of it."

"Tell us," George said. She led her aunt off to the side of the gathering to keep their conversation private.

"It's complicated, but I'll try to explain," Aunt Elizabeth began. "You see, there's an old road

6

that leads from the town green to the outskirts of Fairport. It's narrow and winding—a typical country road.

"There have been several accidents on that road over the years," she went on. "They usually happen at night. If people aren't familiar with the turns and they're driving a bit too fast, they miss the curves and end up tipped over an embankment or bending a fender on a tree.

"But last year there was a terrible accident. A driver hit a bicyclist—a boy named Tommy Connor. He was killed."

Nancy and George sucked in their breaths. "But what does that have to do with bats?" Nancy asked.

"I'm getting to that," Aunt Elizabeth said. "Some people think the road should be widened to protect drivers and cyclists. They've filed a petition with the town to begin the work.

"I'm all for saving people's lives, of course," Aunt Elizabeth continued, "but the problem is, there's an endangered species of bat that lives in a grove of trees right on one of the most dangerous turns. If we widen the road and take down the trees, we'll destroy their habitat and the bats will die."

Nancy nodded. "I think I can see where this is leading."

"The road wideners have also filed a petition with the federal government's Fish and Wildlife Service to allow them to take the trees down," Aunt Elizabeth continued. "So I've gathered together a group of people like me, who want to protect the bats. We need to come up with evidence that proves the bats will die if the trees are taken down. If we can prove that, the federal government will forbid the road widening."

"I've read about this kind of thing in the paper," Nancy said. "Sometimes the disputes get so complicated and difficult that they have to be settled by the United States Supreme Court."

Aunt Elizabeth sighed. "We're hoping to avoid that. But we don't have much time. Our dissenting opinions have to be filed in two days, and I'm not at all sure we have everything we need to make a convincing case. But you can find out all about it at the town meeting we've called for tonight," she concluded.

"A town meeting!" George exclaimed. "I've heard about them," she said, turning to Nancy. "They can get pretty heated."

"Do you have a sense of how most of the people in Fairport feel?" Nancy asked Aunt Elizabeth.

"Folks are pretty much split down the middle," Aunt Elizabeth admitted. "Bats aren't the most warm and cuddly of animals, so most people don't care for them. Some are actually scared of them. They don't understand the important role they play in the natural world."

"I've never been afraid of bats," Nancy said. "But I can't say they're my favorite member of the animal kingdom."

"Well, there you have it," Aunt Elizabeth said with an understanding nod. "I hope you can handle all of this," she said, "because I'm about to become the Batwoman of Fairport." She laughed heartily.

George poked Nancy with her elbow. "Oh boy!" she whispered out of her aunt's earshot. "Aunt E. is at it again."

"But enough of this," Aunt Elizabeth said. "I see there's ice cream, and since it's all in my honor, I'd like to get some before it disappears."

Nancy and George kept pace with Aunt Elizabeth as she walked determinedly through the crowd. They were sure they'd find Bess when they found the ice cream.

They were just about to reach the ice-cream table, when a teenaged girl planted herself in front of Aunt Elizabeth.

"Why, Sarah!" Aunt Elizabeth exclaimed. "How nice to see you. Is your mother here?"

The teenager scowled at Aunt Elizabeth. "Yes, she is," she replied in a low voice. "But don't try to keep me from saying what I have to say to you."

Aunt Elizabeth's eyes widened. "Is something wrong, dear?"

Sarah's face reddened with anger. "You know there is!"

Aunt Elizabeth looked baffled. "I wish I could say that I did," she replied. "Won't you tell me?"

"It's you!" Sarah yelled. "You and those stupid bats!"

Aunt Elizabeth stepped back from Sarah. Nancy could tell George's aunt was perplexed by the sullen young woman in front of her.

"You know my brother died on Old Fairport Road," Sarah said angrily, her hands balled into fists. "Are you trying to make sure that other people die as well?"

Aunt Elizabeth reached out to put her arm around Sarah's shoulder to comfort her, but Sarah pushed it away with a ruthless shove.

"You're one of my mother's best friends. You're the one who helped her through her grief when Tommy died," Sarah said, her voice rising. "And now you're betraying us!" She began to cry with choking sobs. "Doesn't his death mean anything to you?"

"Of course—" Aunt Elizabeth began, but Sarah cut her off.

"You care more about animals than you do about people," Sarah cried in anger. "And I'm going to make you pay for it!"

2

A Dangerous Threat

The small crowd that had gathered around Aunt Elizabeth and Sarah Connor was shocked into silence by Sarah's angry words. Bess appeared and stood to one side, looking puzzled.

A young woman stepped out of the crowd. "I couldn't help overhearing what you said, Sarah." She spoke softly, putting an arm around her. "But you have to understand, it isn't that we don't care about people, it's that we care about the world we all live in."

Sarah brushed her arm aside. "Jessie, I've heard all this before," she said, wiping her eyes with the back of her hand. "It doesn't make sense to me and it never will." She turned abruptly and stalked away.

Aunt Elizabeth's face was pale as she silently watched the girl walk off.

Bess approached her friends. "What happened?" she asked softly.

George shushed her friend. "I'll tell you later," she assured her.

"It's all right, Mrs. Porter," Jessie said, hugging Aunt Elizabeth. "She's just upset."

Aunt Elizabeth shook her head. "I know, but this is one of the few times in my life I've been at a loss for words." A wan smile broke across her face. "She makes me wonder . . ."

The young woman held her hand out to Nancy. "I don't know your name, but I'm Jessie Fein," she said.

"Oh, dear, I'm sorry," Aunt Elizabeth said. "I'm falling down on the job." She quickly introduced Nancy, George, and Bess.

"Jessie is a biology student at Fairport College," Aunt Elizabeth explained. "She's been an enormous help to me on some of my projects. She knows a great deal about animals."

As they chatted, John Stryker, the town manager, joined the group. "I couldn't help but overhear Sarah Connor," he said.

"Oh, John," Aunt Elizabeth said. "What are we going to do?"

He shook his head. "I suppose we'll hash it out at the town meeting tonight."

Aunt Elizabeth introduced him to the girls.

Nancy turned to him. "This sounds like a real controversy," she said.

"You're right," Mr. Stryker agreed. "We don't get them often, but when we do, they tend to be heated," he replied. "That's why the town meetings are so valuable. They let everyone voice their concerns."

"I don't know if it's anything the town itself can decide," Jessie said. "The federal government has very stringent rules about the habitats of endangered species. They can't be disturbed."

Mr. Stryker nodded. "That's what I told those folks who filed the petition to widen the road. Against my wishes, I might add." He gave Aunt Elizabeth a wink. "And even if that weren't true, there isn't any money in the town budget for road improvements this year."

"Oh, John, you know we can always get around that," Aunt Elizabeth reprimanded him mildly.

"In this case, probably not," Mr. Stryker pointed out. "Last winter's snows wiped out the surpluses in several of the funds." He turned to Aunt Elizabeth with a smile. "And usually you'll do a fund-raiser. But this time you're on the other side—luckily."

Aunt Elizabeth straightened her shoulders. "We'll just have to come up with some kind of compromise. Even though I don't want to harm the bats, I can still see Sarah's point."

Mr. Stryker waved and said, "I've got to be off. I'm sure I'll see all of you tonight."

Goodbyes were said all around.

"Would you like to come back to my house for tea?" Aunt Elizabeth asked the girls. "I'm sure I could find some soft drinks if you'd like something less stuffy."

"That would be great," George said to her aunt. "We can unpack our bags and settle in."

"Why don't you follow me back?" Aunt Elizabeth suggested. "I don't think you'd know the way otherwise, George. It's been so long since you were last here."

The three friends and Jessie piled into the rental car. They waited for Aunt Elizabeth to pull out of her parking spot down the block and followed her as she circled the town green and turned down a side road.

Soon enough the green was left behind and the houses became sparser as the road twisted and turned, heading out into the country.

"We're on Old Fairport Road now," Jessie said as Nancy drove. "This is the road that's causing all the trouble."

Nancy gazed at the passing scenery. Trees were just leafing out with the pale green foliage of spring, and clumps of daffodils dotted the side of the road. Nancy expertly negotiated several hairpin turns. She could easily see how the turns could be treacherous, especially at night.

"We're about to reach the place where the bats roost," Jessie told them as the car crossed a small bridge spanning a sparkling stream. She pointed. "See that clump of oaks? Bats love to roost in trees during the day. Those oaks are so tall it keeps them from being disturbed."

Nancy noticed the trees were clustered along the inside of a curve in the road. At night, in the dark, she could imagine what kind of problems the grove of trees could cause. Even in the daytime it was a blind curve.

"How did you get interested in bats?" Nancy asked Jessie, coming out of the turn. "They're such odd creatures."

Jessie chuckled. "Well, they are and they aren't. They're the only mammal that flies."

"What about flying squirrels?" Bess asked.

"Flying squirrels don't have wings," Jessie replied. "They have folds of skin that act like parachutes so they can glide from branch to branch. They can't really fly. But bats really do have wings, like birds, even though they're related to foxes and dogs."

"I never knew that!" Nancy exclaimed.

"In fact, one species of bat is called the flying fox," Jessie said. "Looking at a close-up picture of its face, you would swear that it was a fox."

Nancy followed Aunt Elizabeth's car as it pulled into a winding driveway and came to a stop in front of a dark red colonial house.

"What a pretty home," Nancy said, stepping out of the car. "It looks very old."

"It is," George replied. "It's been in the family for centuries. I think it was built right after the Revolutionary War. Aunt E. and my uncle made some additions, but it's basically the same house it was over two hundred years ago."

"Well, here we are," Aunt Elizabeth said, joining them on the front walk. "Let's get your bags inside and have some refreshments."

She went up the steps and stood beneath a small portico as she pushed open the front door. "We don't use keys here," she said. "Never have."

Nancy, George, and Bess took their luggage out of the trunk and walked through the door that Aunt Elizabeth held open. They stepped into a tiny vestibule. Off to one side was a parlor, to the other a large colonial-era kitchen with a fireplace that took up the better part of one wall. A large round table with captain's chairs gathered around it gave it a homey, inviting air.

"I just love the way old houses smell, don't you?" Bess asked. "Kind of musty and spicy."

"You can take the stairs up," Aunt Elizabeth said, pointing to a steep, narrow flight of stairs in

17

front of them. "I'll let you decide who gets which room. Then come on down. Jessie and I will get the tea ready."

The girls went up the stairs and peeked into each of the rooms. Bess chose the pink one with the canopy bed. George took the blue room with a plaid bedspread and curtains. Nancy decided she liked the yellow room that looked out over the front yard.

When they went back downstairs, Nancy noted that Jessie and Aunt Elizabeth had kept their promise. On a tray on a low table in the parlor was a pot of tea, cookies, and bottles of cola.

The parlor was furnished with a comfortable couch facing some easy chairs, all covered in flowery, faded chintz. A curtained window looked out over the side yard. The girls settled into the chairs as Aunt Elizabeth poured tea, passed out drinks, and then sat on the couch next to Jessie.

They chatted about Fairport and some of George's more distant relatives who lived nearby, but when the conversation lapsed for a moment, Nancy brought up the subject of bats.

"Jessie, I've heard you say that bats are important in the balance of nature, but I have to admit I don't know why," she said. "Could you tell us?"

Jessie put down the tea she had been sipping

and turned to Nancy with an eager smile. "Bats perform a number of functions in the natural world," she said. "One of the most important, as far as we're concerned, is that the bats in Fairport eat insects like mosquitoes. If they didn't, we wouldn't be able to bear being outside day or night. We'd be bitten to death."

Nancy laughed. "It's funny to hear that, since so many people think bats suck blood. Instead they protect us from the critters that do."

"There are so many myths and legends about bats that aren't true," Jessie said. "For instance, many people think bats are ferocious and attack people, but nothing could be further from the truth. Bats are actually gentle creatures who like to be left alone. Unless you're an insect, they'll steer clear."

"Why do these myths persist?" George asked. "Why are people so afraid of bats?"

"Because bats are nocturnal," Jessie answered, "meaning they go out at night. That makes them kind of creepy. They squeak when they fly— that's the sound they make to help them navigate by sonar—and it can be an eerie sound. But I guess the scariest thing is that when people get close enough to see them, bats bare their teeth in defense. It's not a pretty sight."

Everyone laughed.

"Are they really endangered?" Bess asked.

Jessie nodded. "More than half of all the bat species in America are endangered or threatened. I could tell you horrible stories about people who have murdered thousands and thousands of bats roosting in caves—simply out of fear and ignorance. Other colonies of bats are killed when people cut down the trees where they like to roost. That's what we're fighting here in Fairport."

"I've never realized how interesting bats are," Nancy said.

The phone rang on a small parlor table, and Aunt Elizabeth rose to answer it. The girls chatted quietly as Aunt Elizabeth picked up the receiver and said hello.

But out of the corner of her eye, Nancy saw Aunt Elizabeth's face go white as she listened to what the caller had to say. Dropping the receiver into the cradle, Aunt Elizabeth collapsed into a chair.

"Aunt E., what is it?" George asked. She leaped up and dashed over to her aunt's side. "Who was it?"

Aunt Elizabeth clasped her hands in her lap and shook her head. "I don't know who it was," she replied, her voice low and frightened. "All I know is, I was told that if I continue to try to save the bats, I'll be just as endangered as they are!"

3

Fly-by-night

"But who would want to threaten you like that?" George asked, putting a hand on her aunt's shoulder.

Aunt Elizabeth shook her head. "I don't know. We've had controversies in Fairport before, but we've always worked them out." She paused for a moment and rubbed her temple with a shaky hand. "I don't like this."

"Did you recognize the voice?" Nancy asked.

Aunt Elizabeth shook her head. "It was muffled. I think the caller tried to disguise it."

That was usually the case, Nancy thought.

Aunt Elizabeth rose. "Well, I do know one thing," she said. "I won't be bullied. Whoever called is going to have a fight on their hands."

"And you know we're behind you one hundred percent," George said, as the others agreed.

They had settled back to continue their conversation when the doorbell rang.

"If it's not one thing, it's another," Aunt Elizabeth grumbled as she went to the door.

When she returned it was with another woman, whom she introduced as Margaret Connor, Sarah's mother.

Mrs. Connor sat down on the edge of a chair across from Aunt Elizabeth. She twisted a handkerchief nervously.

"Margaret, won't you have some tea?" Aunt Elizabeth asked.

Mrs. Connor shook her head. "No, but thank you, Elizabeth." She straightened her shoulders and said, "I've come to ask you a favor."

Aunt Elizabeth leaned forward on the sofa. "You know I'll do whatever I can. We've been friends for a very long time."

Mrs. Connor cleared her throat. "I saw Sarah when she returned from your celebration. She was very upset."

"I know," Aunt Elizabeth said sympathetically. "She has strong feelings about the road widening."

"I don't know what to think, to be honest with you." Mrs. Connor wrung her handkerchief and said softly, "She hasn't been right since Tommy died. She worshipped her older brother. His death was an enormous loss."

Aunt Elizabeth leaned over and patted Mrs. Connor's hand. "I know, Margaret, it was a great loss to you as well. To everyone in Fairport."

"She's struggled to make sense of it," Mrs. Connor said with great anguish. "But the only way she can deal with it is to try to keep what happened to Tommy from happening to anyone else."

Aunt Elizabeth spoke gently. "I can see why widening the road is so important to her. It's become a kind of mission, hasn't it?"

Mrs. Connor nodded. "I've always said that Sarah is all heart. She takes things so hard. I'm very worried about her."

"Of course you are," Aunt Elizabeth said comfortingly. "What mother wouldn't be?"

Mrs. Connor looked at her friend with pleading eyes. "Isn't there any way you can change your mind?"

All eyes were on Aunt Elizabeth.

She sighed. "Margaret, if I could, I would. You know I'd do whatever I could to keep Sarah from being so unhappy."

"Then stop this silly crusade for those wretched bats!" Mrs. Connor exclaimed.

Aunt Elizabeth shook her head. "I can't, Margaret. It's an important issue. The bats are a part of the ecosystem here. What's more, they have a right to live undisturbed."

"But what about people!" Mrs. Connor said forcefully. "Don't they have a right to travel on that road safely?"

"They do," Aunt Elizabeth said, "but not at the expense of the life of another creature." She picked up her teacup and then put it down again. "I'm hoping we'll be able to reach a compromise."

"What would it be?" Mrs. Connor asked anxiously.

"I don't know," Aunt Elizabeth admitted, "but until then, I have to take a position. And my position is against the road widening."

"That's your final word?" Mrs. Connor asked.

"Yes. I'm sorry, but it is," Aunt Elizabeth responded firmly.

Mrs. Connor rose to leave. "Then that's that, I suppose."

Aunt Elizabeth stood up. "Margaret, you know how much I love you and Sarah. Trust me, it will all work out. Until then, it's going to be difficult. But let's not lose our friendship in the process."

Mrs. Connor turned to Aunt Elizabeth. "Of course, you're right," she admitted, and threw her arms around her friend. She and Aunt Elizabeth hugged.

"Please tell Sarah what I've told you and reassure her that I'm willing to compromise," Aunt Elizabeth said.

Aunt Elizabeth saw her friend to the door and then returned to the parlor.

"This is hard for you, isn't it, Aunt E.?" George asked.

"It is," Aunt Elizabeth agreed. "But let's not dwell on it." She brushed a stray wisp of hair off her forehead. "Let's see what you can do with the rest of your day."

It was late afternoon, and the sun streamed through a west-facing window in Aunt Elizabeth's parlor.

Nancy spoke up. "I was hoping we could visit the grove where the bats live. I'd like to see that part of the road before the meeting tonight."

"That's a good idea," Jessie said. "The only problem is, we can't park a car on the roadside. There isn't enough room. And it's too far to walk."

"Why don't you take bicycles?" Aunt Elizabeth suggested. She turned to George. "When your cousins went off to college, they left their bikes behind. I think they're still in the garage. They may be a little dusty and creaky, but they'll get you there."

Nancy frowned. "The only thing I worry about is biking on that road," she said. "Wouldn't we be in danger?"

Aunt Elizabeth shook her head. "I don't think

so. As long as you return before dark, you'll be safe."

A trip out to the garage revealed four three-speed bicycles leaning against the back wall. Nancy, George, Bess, and Jessie each took one and set off down Aunt Elizabeth's driveway.

The sun was still warm, and it was refreshing to be outdoors. With Jessie in the lead, they followed the road as it twisted and turned for about a mile and a half. When Jessie motioned to the other three, they pulled over to the left-hand side.

The grove of oaks nestled in a corner of the road. Leaning their bikes against the tree trunks, the girls gathered on a rocky outcrop in the woods to their right.

"What kind of bats live here?" Nancy asked Jessie.

"Gray bats," Jessie said, "a species that's been endangered for a while. It's unusual to find a colony up here. That's why they have to be saved."

Bess looked up into the trees. "Would we be able to see them from here? Or do they camouflage themselves?"

"That's a good question," Jessie said to Bess. "Their coloring protects them because the trees they roost in, like these oaks, have gray bark. Right now they're just coming out of their winter hibernation. We suspect there must be a cave nearby, because that's where they hibernate, but we haven't found one yet."

"How did you discover they were here?" Nancy asked.

"Martin Noble, a professor at my college who's an expert on bats, goes out regularly at night to sight them," Jessie said. "He was here around twilight one evening and saw them flitting from tree to tree."

"Did he catch one?" George asked.

"Yes," Jessie said. "That's what set off the controversy. When he heard about the petition, he caught one for proof."

"How do you catch a bat?" Nancy asked.

"Do you have to have a long-handled net or something?" Bess asked. "Like catching butterflies?"

"Not exactly," Jessie said, laughing. "You stretch some soft nets between the trees. It doesn't harm them at all."

The sun was beginning to set. The trees cast long shadows on the mossy ground.

"If we wait a few more minutes, we might see them head out for their evening snack," Jessie said. "Let's sit quietly."

The girls sat on the rock and gazed up expectantly.

Nancy looked around her. As the sun began to

dip below the horizon, the wind died down and the woods became quiet. She heard a rustling overhead and saw a small darting shape take flight.

"It looks like a bird," Bess said.

"Yes, but it flies differently and faster," Jessie replied.

As Nancy watched, she saw several other darting shapes flitting from tree to tree.

In the quiet twilight, the young women could hear the rustling of wings and the high-pitched squeak of the bats' sonar as they set out for the night.

"It's strange and beautiful at the same time, isn't it?" Nancy whispered. Everyone nodded, awed by the sight.

Suddenly a gruff male voice disturbed the silence: "What are you doing here?"

Nancy turned to her right and saw a middle-aged man standing at the edge of the grove. He had graying brown hair and a closely clipped beard ending in a sharp point. He was dressed completely in black.

"I'm sorry," Nancy said. "Were we disturbing you?"

"You're not disturbing me, but you're trespassing on my property," the man said brusquely.

"I thought this was public property," Nancy said. "Who are you?"

28

"My name is Hank Tolchinsky," he said. "I have a house further back in the woods, but this is my property, from the rock on. I wish you'd leave."

"We were watching the bats," Jessie told him. "I suppose you know about the proposal to widen the road."

The man laughed harshly. "I'm well aware of it. I don't like bats. Never have. I wish they weren't here. Mostly because I've been getting a lot of snoopers trampling all over my property."

"We'll leave then," Jessie said quietly. "And we're sorry we trespassed."

Nancy observed the man closely. There was something about him that seemed sinister, as if he had something to hide.

"Will you be coming to the town meeting tonight?" she asked him. "If you feel that strongly about the bats, you should."

The man gave her a long look. "I may. I may not. I don't like the bats, as I've said. But I also don't want a lot of road equipment here making noise and disturbing my solitude. Now, if you don't mind, please leave." He turned on his heel and left as quietly as he'd come.

Nancy and her friends retrieved their bikes and hopped on them. Nancy looked behind her as she pedaled away and saw that Mr. Tolchinsky had returned to the rocky outcrop. He was watching them with an inscrutable look on his face.

Nancy steered her bike over to Jessie's and said, "Not very nice, is he?"

Jessie gave Nancy a look. "He's creepy."

Nancy held back to let Jessie assume the lead again, and then quickened her pedaling to keep up as Jessie sped ahead. Night was falling and soon it would be dangerous to be out on the road.

But as Nancy headed around the last turn before Aunt Elizabeth's driveway, a thought flitted through her mind. At first, she had thought Sarah had probably made that phone call to Aunt Elizabeth. Now she wondered if there wasn't someone else who wanted to stop Aunt Elizabeth's crusade for the bats as well.

4

Hanging by a Threat

When Nancy and the three girls got back to Aunt Elizabeth's, dinner was ready in the big kitchen. She had prepared roast chicken with stuffing, baked potatoes, and green beans.

"I thought you might be hungry after your bike trip," Aunt Elizabeth said. "Wash up and then we'll eat."

The kitchen, with its big round table, gingham curtains, and old copper pots hanging in the huge unlit fireplace, was cozily lit by a wrought iron fixture above the table and candles glowing on the mantel. The young women chatted excitedly, taking turns washing their hands at the sink.

At last they sat down and began to pass the serving dishes.

"What a feast!" Bess said. "I'm starving."

"Tell me about your adventure," Aunt Elizabeth said, addressing George. "I'm guessing something exciting must have happened from all the chatter I overheard."

"Do you know Hank Tolchinsky?" George asked her aunt, as she passed the green beans to Nancy.

Aunt Elizabeth's eyebrows shot up. "Know him? I should say I do! He's an odd one, that's for sure."

"How so?" Nancy asked.

"He moved here a couple of years ago, and he's been a real mystery man," Aunt Elizabeth said, placing the bowl of stuffing in the center of the table. "Most people who move to Fairport become involved in at least one or two of the town's doings. We're very civic-minded here." She paused to pass the gravy to Jessie.

"But not Hank Tolchinsky," Aunt Elizabeth continued. "I went to his house when he first arrived and asked him if he wanted to contribute to the town beautification fund. He slammed the door in my face!"

"That's rude," Nancy said.

Aunt Elizabeth nodded. "I thought so too. He called me a meddling busybody when I asked what brought him to Fairport. Usually people are happy to tell you why they came."

"So he knows you?" Nancy asked.

Aunt Elizabeth laughed. "If one rude encounter means knowing someone, then I suppose he does."

"Hmmm," Nancy murmured. She crunched a green bean, lost in thought.

"Nancy," George said, observing her friend. "I know when your mind is working, and right now I'd say it's working overtime."

Nancy put down her fork. "It just seems to me that Mr. Tolchinsky must have something to hide," she said. "Why would he slam the door on Aunt Elizabeth? Why was he so adamant about getting us off his property? Clearly, none of us meant any harm."

"I think I know what you're getting at, Nancy," George said. "Are you thinking he might have been the one who made that threatening phone call to Aunt E.?"

"I'm not sure," Nancy said. "The logical suspect would be Sarah. But since Mr. Tolchinsky knows Aunt Elizabeth and has made it clear he doesn't like bats . . ."

Aunt Elizabeth stood up and started to clear the table. "You can't exactly call me Ms. Popularity right now, can you?"

The others laughed and rose to help her. They had just finished scraping and rinsing the dishes for the dishwasher when the doorbell rang.

"That must be Professor Noble," Aunt Elizabeth said on her way to the door. "He said he'd stop by to go with us to the meeting."

They crowded into the vestibule while Aunt Elizabeth greeted her visitor.

"This is Professor Martin Noble," she said, introducing him to Nancy, Bess, and George. "He teaches at Fairport College and knows everything there is to know about bats."

Professor Noble was a tall man with dark brown skin, close-clipped black hair, and a genial, intelligent-looking face.

"Are you ready for tonight?" he asked Aunt Elizabeth.

"I am, but I'm a little reluctant to speak," Aunt Elizabeth said. She led him into the parlor and motioned for him to sit on the couch next to her. Nancy and her friends settled into their chairs. Then Elizabeth told him about Sarah's angry confrontation after the ceremony.

"It's harder to stand firm when you can understand the other side of the argument," Professor Noble said.

"That's right," Aunt Elizabeth said, "especially since Sarah's mother came over this afternoon begging me to change my mind."

Professor Noble sighed. "You're really caught in the middle, aren't you?"

Aunt Elizabeth went on to tell him about the

34

threatening phone call she'd received that afternoon. Then she asked Nancy to describe her encounter with Hank Tolchinsky, which Nancy did.

Professor Noble frowned.

"Do you know him?" Nancy asked.

"I had the same run-in with him that you did while I was observing the bats," Professor Noble said. "Not a particularly nice character, but he is within his rights to want us off his land if we're trespassing."

"That's a diplomatic answer," Aunt Elizabeth said. They all laughed.

When the laughter died down, Nancy spoke up. "Could you tell me how you got involved in this?" she asked Professor Noble. "I've heard that a petition has been made to the Fish and Wildlife Service, but I'm not sure how it works."

"I'll be glad to explain," Professor Noble said, smiling. "It's not complicated."

Nancy settled into her comfortable chair, wanting to hear everything he said so she could be prepared for the meeting that evening.

"A couple of months ago," Professor Noble began, "some people in Fairport decided that Old Fairport Road needed to be widened. I suppose you've heard about the accidents? And what happened to Tommy Connor?"

Nancy nodded.

Professor Noble went on. "A motion was raised at a town meeting to look into the possibility of widening the road. Mrs. Porter posed the question that conservationists always ask when changes are going to be made to the environment: Would the changes affect the animals or plants that live there? No one knew. But the motion passed, even though John Stryker tried to get enough support to keep it from passing."

"I've never understood why he was against the road widening," Aunt Elizabeth broke in. "Usually I have to fight him tooth and nail on conservation issues."

Professor Noble nodded and went on. "And so Mrs. Porter called and asked me to do a quick biological assessment of the area. That's when I discovered the gray bats."

Aunt Elizabeth excused herself to make coffee. "Keep going," she said, leaving the room. "I've heard this before."

"When I let the town council know I had found bats, and endangered bats at that, there was an uproar," he continued. "In order to widen the road, the town council had to file a petition with the U.S. Fish and Wildlife Service for what they call an Incidental Take permit. They'd have to prove that taking down those trees wasn't going to endanger the bats' habitat."

"Will it?" Nancy asked.

"I think it will," Professor Noble said. "But the town called in some experts from the state fish and game agency to help them prepare the permit application and develop a habitat conservation plan."

"Do they think they can take the trees down without endangering the bats?" George asked.

"They do, but I think they're wrong," Professor Noble said. "That's why I'm going to the meeting tonight. To give my side of the story."

"Why is taking down a clump of trees so devastating to the bats?" Nancy asked. "Aren't there other trees?"

"Those tall oaks are the only kind of tree for miles around where they can roost," Noble explained. "They won't roost in smaller trees. I also suspect there's a cave nearby where they hibernate for the winter. Otherwise they wouldn't be where they are.

"But thanks to Mr. Tolchinsky," he said with a wry grin, "I haven't been able to find the cave. For all we know, it could be in the path of the road widening. If it is, then we have a much more solid case to preserve the land as it is for the sake of the bats. But I only have two more days to find it."

"Why is that?" Nancy asked.

"Because the deadline for filing the petition to prevent the road work is two days from now."

"And then what happens?" Nancy asked again.

"The Fish and Wildlife Service reviews the application and makes a decision. Usually it doesn't take them very long. But in a case like this, where there are serious objections, it can sometimes go on for years."

"Please don't say that." Aunt Elizabeth came back in with a tray of coffee, cups, and a strudel.

When everyone was settled with dessert, Nancy asked Professor Noble something she'd been wondering about. "How did you get interested in bats?"

Professor Noble put down his cup. "When I was a child, we lived in a house at the top of a hill. In the backyard were a couple of old oaks. At twilight my parents and I used to sit out on the back porch and watch the bats take flight for the evening."

"Sounds a little spooky to me," Bess said with a laugh.

"Kind of," Professor Noble said, smiling. "My parents weren't naturalists, but they had a great appreciation for the natural world and all its inhabitants. And I've found I developed a lot of sympathy for bats. They're like the underdogs of the natural world. Few people understand how important they are."

Aunt Elizabeth looked at the clock on the mantel. "We should go now," she told the group.

Bess began to collect the dishes, but Aunt Elizabeth said, "Leave the dishes where they are. There's going to be quite a crowd, and if we want to find a good parking spot, we'll have to get there early."

As they hurried to get ready, the doorbell rang. "Now, who could that be?" Aunt Elizabeth said. She headed for the door.

Nancy heard her open the door and then a piercing scream. She rushed into the vestibule and found Aunt Elizabeth collapsed against the door frame, her hand on her chest.

"What is it?" Nancy asked, putting an arm around her.

Aunt Elizabeth pointed out the door. Hanging from a rafter of the portico was a bat, twisting in the night breeze.

Pinned to it was a note. In bold square letters it said: Stop! Or you'll be hanging next!

5

An Angry Meeting

Nancy stepped out onto the porch and studied the bat in the dim glow of the overhead light. Then she tugged on the string and pulled it down.

"Ugh!" Bess cried. "Nancy, how could you?"

"Is it dead?" George asked.

Holding the dangling bat in front of her, Nancy went into the vestibule. Aunt Elizabeth sat on a straight-backed chair, with Jessie holding her hand.

"It's not a real bat, Aunt E.," Nancy said. "It's a stuffed toy."

"Thank goodness," Aunt Elizabeth said with a harried sigh. She took the bat from Nancy and turned it over. "Kind of cute," she said, "except for that nasty note."

Taking it gently from Aunt Elizabeth's hands, Nancy brought the bat into the kitchen and

placed it on the table. Studying the fuzzy creature, she tried to decide what to do next. Should
she leave the note as it was and call the police to
have them dust it for fingerprints?

Whoever had left the bat was probably not a
criminal. Even if the police found some prints,
there would be no way to match them up if the
prints' owner had no police record.

She removed the pin from the note and held
the paper by its edges. The letters were blocky
and well-formed, and appeared to be written
with a felt-tip marker. The message was written
on common lined paper. No way to trace that.

The bat itself was as big around as her hand,
with velvety wings and a silvery plush body. In a
child's hands it would have been cute, but here it
seemed to eye her malevolently.

Bess, George, and Professor Noble joined
Nancy in the kitchen.

"I hear you're a detective," Professor Noble
said. "It appears you've got your first clue."

"I can't do much with the note," Nancy said,
"but I may be able to trace the bat." She fingered
the label sewn into a seam on its back.

Aunt Elizabeth and Jessie came into the
kitchen.

"Shouldn't we call the police?" Professor Noble asked. "This is a death threat."

"No," Aunt Elizabeth said firmly. "If Sarah's

doing this, then it's the work of a frightened child, not a criminal. We'll let it go for the time being."

She pulled a jacket off a hook near the kitchen door. "We've got a meeting to go to," she said, jamming her arms into her jacket sleeves. "Who's riding with me?"

"Let me drive," George said to her aunt.

Aunt Elizabeth shook her head. "I'm fine, and the driving will calm me down."

Outside, they divided into two groups. Nancy, Bess, and George went with Aunt Elizabeth. Jessie hopped into the car with Professor Noble.

On the way, Nancy noticed how tensely Aunt Elizabeth's hands were gripping the steering wheel. Her heart went out to her. The woman was only trying to do what she felt was right, and look what had happened!

Even though they were half an hour early, cars were already circling the green looking for parking spots. Aunt Elizabeth found a spot not too far from the Town Hall, a brick building capped with a clock tower.

When they reached the steps in front of the Town Hall, Nancy could feel the excitement of the people crowded behind her and her friends. They followed the movement of the crowd into a large, square room set up with folding chairs. A

42

long table stretched across the front of the room, already filled with members of the town council.

Nancy and her friends found a row of seats toward the front of the hall and sat down. A few minutes later she saw Professor Noble and Jessie come in and stand off to one side. Mrs. Connor and Sarah entered shortly afterward and, Nancy suspected, deliberately chose to stand on the other side of the room.

Finally, a woman at the front of the room banged a gavel. "Who's that?" Nancy whispered to Aunt Elizabeth.

"That's Jeannette Oberdorf," Aunt Elizabeth murmured. "She's the town secretary."

"As you all know, we're here to talk about the widening of Old Fairport Road," Ms. Oberdorf said, raising her voice until the crowd quieted down. "We've filed a petition with the United States government to allow us to alter what appears to be land that harbors an endangered species of bat. Now is the time for those who object to the road widening to say their piece."

Nancy saw Mr. Stryker look around the crowd. His eyes rested on Aunt Elizabeth for a long time. Was he expecting her to speak up first for the conservationists?

Professor Noble walked over and took the microphone set up in the center aisle.

"I'm Martin Noble," he began. "I teach biology at Fairport College, and I'd like to register my objection to the widening of Old Fairport Road."

Groans were heard around the room.

Ms. Oberdorf banged her gavel again. "I want to remind everyone that we're here to listen. Give Professor Noble a chance to speak."

"Thank you," Professor Noble said. "I know many of you are in favor of widening the road and couldn't care less about bats."

Some of the people laughed nervously.

"But what if we were talking about deer?" he asked. "Or fluffy little bunnies?"

People murmured.

"Bats aren't the cuddliest of animals," he went on.

"Hear, hear!" cried a voice from the crowd. Everyone laughed.

"But they're vitally important," Professor Noble said when people had settled down again. "Bats keep the insect population down in Fairport. If they didn't, you'd be tortured by mosquitoes even more than you are now on a warm, summer evening."

"So what?" someone called.

Nancy turned to George and raised her eyebrows. Fairporters were a feisty bunch!

Professor Noble frowned. " 'So what?' you ask? We're all connected to the natural world. Bats may not seem important to you, but in the natural world they play a vital role. Lose them, and you could begin to lose the plants and animals you care about."

The professor went back to his place by the wall. A tall, sandy-haired man rose and took the microphone.

"I'm Chuck Danzig," he said, "from the state fish and game office. I've done a biological survey of the area, and I believe taking down those trees won't destroy the bats' habitat."

Professor Noble went back to the microphone.

"Chuck, I've seen your conservation plan, and I agree with you—up to a point," Professor Noble said. "You're not taking into account that bats hibernate during the winter. There's a cave near the trees where they do that now.

"I know you think you can relocate the bats to a clump of trees a couple of miles away," he continued. "But there's no cave there. Without a cave they'll die when it gets cold."

"What cave?" Mr. Danzig asked. "Find it, and then we'll have something to talk about." He left the microphone and sat down.

"We're going to look for it tomorrow," Professor Noble replied, and went back to stand beside Jessie.

Ms. Oberdorf scanned the crowd. "Would anyone else like to speak?" she asked.

People turned in their chairs to see who would

step forward. To Nancy's surprise, Mr. Tolchin-sky went up to the microphone.

He cleared his throat. "My name is Hank Tolchinsky, and I'm somewhat new to Fairport," he began quietly. "I have to say I've never seen so much fuss about so little."

People moved restlessly in their chairs. Aunt Elizabeth sat up and glared at him.

"I couldn't care less about those bats," the man continued. "And I couldn't care less about the road widening. In fact, I've read about a town where a road was widened, and all it did was encourage people to drive even faster and more recklessly because they thought they had more space to maneuver in."

Angry murmuring began in the hall.

"But that's not my concern," Tolchinsky continued, raising his hand and pointing at the crowd. "All I care about is people staying off my property," he declared. "I'm sick and tired of finding strangers wandering around on my land looking for bats and who knows what else. I came here for peace and quiet. And I'll do whatever I have to to get it!" He turned on his heel and stormed out of the hall.

"How rude!" Aunt Elizabeth exclaimed. All around them voices buzzed in anger.

Sarah rushed to the microphone and began to speak, her face twisted with emotion. "Is this the

46

kind of thing we have to hear? All he's concerned about is his privacy. What about my brother? He lost his life on that road because it was too narrow and dark and someone misjudged how far away Tommy was from their car."

Sarah began to cry.

"The only thing I can agree with Mr. Tolchinsky about is that I hate those bats, too. And I think anyone who supports the bats and goes against the road widening is a murderer!" She glared at Aunt Elizabeth, then walked away from the microphone.

Mr. Stryker, who had been watching the proceedings from his seat at the front table, stood up and grabbed the microphone from Ms. Oberdorf.

"Please, let's all quiet down," he said. "We've held this meeting so that different points of view can be heard—not to call names."

Nancy saw Mrs. Connor holding Sarah back from the microphone.

"Anyone who has information they think should be filed along with the petition to the Fish and Wildlife Service should make sure to give it to Jeannette by the day after tomorrow," said Mr. Stryker. "Unless someone else has something to say, I'm going to suggest we close this meeting."

The crowd was dead quiet. Then Aunt Elizabeth stood up and went to the microphone.

"As you all know, I've been an ardent conservationist for years," she said. "And I've fought many a hard fight for causes I thought were just." She paused. "But this is the hardest one I've ever had to fight because I'm not entirely sure I'm right."

"That's news to us," someone said. A few people laughed.

"All I know," Aunt Elizabeth said, "is that we can't afford to compromise the biological diversity of our world any more than we can afford to compromise the safety of Fairport's citizens."

"Bravo!" cried someone in the crowd.

Mr. Stryker took the microphone again. "I think we've heard all we need to hear tonight. I'm familiar with the circumstances Mr. Tolchinsky described. Wide roads can be hazardous. But it's time to pass on our comments to the federal government, and let it decide."

There was some grumbling in the crowd, but when Mr. Stryker asked that the meeting be adjourned, he was quickly seconded.

Nancy and her friends moved slowly with the crowd toward the door.

"I've never known that man to be so accommodating to the environmentalists' point of view before," Aunt Elizabeth said under her breath.

"What do you think it means?" Nancy asked as she dodged a chair to head out the door.

48

"I don't know." Aunt Elizabeth shook her head. "It's just odd."

Outside the Town Hall the crowd was still milling about. People seemed reluctant to leave.

Professor Noble asked Aunt Elizabeth whether he could drive her home. "I have some things to discuss with you on the way."

Aunt Elizabeth agreed to go with him. "George can take my car and drive everyone else home." She waved goodbye and headed off with Professor Noble.

A few minutes later, as George maneuvered the car out of the parking spot, Bess spoke up.

"I guess we've heard from all sides now," she said. "What a predicament!"

"You're right, Bess," Nancy said from the backseat. "But what bothers me is that nothing anyone said at that meeting gave me any solid clues as to who could be calling Aunt Elizabeth or leaving threatening notes. Sarah is the logical suspect, I suppose. And Mr. Tolchinsky might be mean enough to do it, too. But it's still not clear in my mind."

"Is it time to call in the police?" George asked.

"It might be," Nancy said. "Let's see what tomorrow brings."

As they drove along Old Fairport Road, Nancy mulled the situation over. Sarah was open about her hostility toward Aunt Elizabeth, and Mr.

Tolchinsky was certainly open about his hostility toward the townspeople. But their openness, in an ironic way, made them less suspect, unless they were devious and manipulative enough to use reverse psychology.

"It sure is dark on this road," George said. She made a sharp turn, tires skidding on the loose gravel of the shoulder. Nancy heard the answering skid of another set of tires behind them. Looking back to see how close the car was, she saw the dim shape of a vehicle. The car did not have its headlights on.

"I think we're being followed," she said to George.

George looked in the rearview mirror. "I don't see any lights," she said.

"I know, but I made out the shape of a car," Nancy said.

"Look!" Bess cried. She pointed out the window.

A car had pulled alongside and was keeping pace with them. Its headlights were still off. George pressed down on the accelerator, trying to go faster and lose the car, but it matched their speed.

Another bend in the road lay ahead, and the mysterious car was edging them toward the shoulder. They were almost at the grove of oaks where the bats lived.

"Watch out for the trees!" Bess said urgently.

Nancy looked through the windshield and saw the trees come rushing up, closer and closer, as they approached the sharp curve. George was still trying to get away from the car beside her. She again hit the gas pedal, but the car kept pace with her.

The grove of trees loomed up in front of them. Bess let out a cry of fear.

With only seconds to spare, Nancy shouted, "Hit the brakes, George!"

6

Secrets Overheard

George slammed on the brakes, bringing the car to a halt only inches before it hit the trees. The mystery car sped off into the night.

"What in the world was that?" George asked in a shaky voice, her hands still gripping the steering wheel.

"Somebody must be crazy to drive without headlights!" Bess exclaimed.

"Crazy, perhaps," Nancy said. "But crazy or not, it must have been someone who knows this road like the back of his hand."

"You're right," George said grimly. She pulled onto the road and continued to Aunt Elizabeth's.

Aunt Elizabeth was waiting up for them in the parlor. She listened to what had happened and sighed.

"They must have thought you were me since

you were driving my car," she said. "Please be more careful from now on. I'm not sure what we're dealing with here."

It had been a long day. The girls went up to bed, saying their goodnights in the hallway.

The next day dawned cool and sunny. After a leisurely breakfast of scrambled eggs and English muffins, Nancy, Bess, and George sat with Aunt Elizabeth in the cheerful kitchen and went over the previous day's events, ending with the near "accident" on Old Fairport Road.

"It was terrible," Bess said with a shudder.

"What were they hoping to accomplish?" Aunt Elizabeth asked.

"To scare you," George said. "As you said, since it was your car, they probably thought you were in it."

"But anyone who knows me knows I can't be budged once I take a stand on something," Aunt Elizabeth pointed out. "So it's rather silly."

Nancy couldn't help but think that it might be silly, but it was also dangerous. Was Aunt Elizabeth safe?

"And Mr. Tolchinsky is just about the most unpleasant man I've ever run into!" Aunt Elizabeth exclaimed. "Why bother coming to a town where people care about what goes on if all you want is to be left alone?"

"I wonder if he would threaten people who disturb his peace," George said.

"That's just what I've been thinking," Nancy said. "He knows Aunt Elizabeth and he knows how she feels about the bats. If he thought she was standing in his way . . ."

"But what about Sarah?" Aunt Elizabeth asked. "She seems so unstable. I hate to think someone I've known and loved since she was a baby could do such a thing."

"Should we call in the police?" Nancy asked Aunt Elizabeth. "After all, your life has been threatened."

Aunt Elizabeth gave Nancy a long look. "If it's Sarah making those threats, I don't have to worry, do I? It's childish revenge—nothing serious."

"Perhaps," Nancy admitted. "But as you said, she does appear to be unstable. Angry people can do angry things."

"If it isn't Sarah, if it's Mr. Tolchinsky or someone else we haven't even considered yet, then we don't know who or what we're dealing with, do we?" Aunt Elizabeth replied.

Nancy and her friends murmured in agreement.

"I just don't want to get Sarah into trouble if it's just a *prank*," Aunt Elizabeth finally said. "Is that foolish of me?"

"No," Nancy said. "But if it isn't just childish pranks, you could get hurt."

Aunt Elizabeth thought for a moment. "Let's wait," she finally said. "It's only been one day. If something else happens, we'll talk to Gerri Spinetti. She's an officer with the Fairport police, and I've known her for a long time. I'd feel comfortable talking to her."

Nancy agreed with Aunt Elizabeth's plan. She understood why she might want to protect Sarah. She only hoped the threats would end.

"And now let's talk about what you three can do today," Aunt Elizabeth suggested.

After considering several different options, the girls decided to return to the town green and stroll through the shopping district on Main Street.

"There's a nice little coffee shop where you can have lunch," Aunt Elizabeth suggested as they headed out. "And they have the most wonderful pies."

Bess's eyes lit up. "Do you think they have apple pie?" she asked. "And do you think they serve it with whipped cream?"

"Only if you ask," George said dryly.

With that, the girls piled into the car and headed into town.

From the looks of things, Saturday morning was

a major shopping day for the residents of Fairport. People crowded the sidewalks, and Nancy had to circle several times around the green before she could find a parking spot.

She pulled in next to a pickup truck in front of a hardware store. The store looked shabby. The windows held an assortment of old lawn mowers and power tools beneath a thick layer of dust. A note on the door said the owner would return after lunch.

"You'd think a hardware store would do better business than this," Nancy remarked as she got out of the car. "I wonder if those big chain stores aren't cutting into its business?"

They soon were in the middle of the flow of shoppers on Main Street. They strolled and window-shopped, admiring some hand-thrown pottery on display in the window of one store. A poster taped to the window announced that a crafts fair would be held on the green the next day.

"Maybe we should hold on to our spending money until tomorrow," George suggested.

"That's not a bad idea," Nancy agreed. "I'd like to bring something back for Hannah. You know how much she enjoys little presents from my travels."

Hannah Gruen was the Drews' housekeeper back in River Heights. Since Nancy's mother had died when she was young, Hannah had taken care of Nancy and her father, Carson Drew, a lawyer, and was considered a member of the family.

"Oh," Bess sighed. "Look at that dress!"

Nancy and George looked where she pointed. In the window of an expensive boutique was a long and flowing flowered dress whose pastel colors would look perfect with Bess's blond hair and blue eyes.

"Why don't you try it on?" Nancy said. "We can wait for you out here."

Bess eagerly entered the store. Nancy and George saw the shop owner take the dress out of the window for Bess.

"We'll be here for a while," George said.

Nancy laughed. For Bess, trying on clothing almost always turned into a situation fraught with decisions. Nancy liked clothing as much as Bess did and enjoyed being fashionable. She just had a clearer sense of her own style and what she liked. Bess was always willing to experiment.

As Nancy waited, she noticed a stack of newspapers in a rack next to the door of the store. A headline caught her eye: "Mild Winter Heralds Early Spring."

Something about it tugged at her memory. Then she remembered. Hadn't Mr. Stryker said the winter had been so harsh that it had depleted the town's budget for snow removal?

Before she could think about it further, she saw a man entering the coffee shop several doors down. "Isn't that Mr. Stryker?" she asked George.

"Yes," George said, looking over. "He's someone we should talk to. He might have some ideas about who could be threatening Aunt Elizabeth. After all, he knows everyone in town."

"That's a great idea," Nancy replied. "When Bess is done, we'll have lunch. Maybe we could talk to him then."

In a shorter time than they thought possible, Nancy and George were rejoined by Bess, who shook her head as she left the store.

"I wish I'd seen the price tag before I tried it on," she said. "It was even more expensive than it looked." She sighed. "I guess I'll drown my sorrows in a burger and some fries."

"Let's have lunch at the coffee shop," Nancy said. "Is that close enough for you?" she added, teasing her friend.

The girls entered the shop and sat down in the last empty booth.

Mr. Stryker was in the booth behind theirs, his back to them. He was deep in conversation with a man across from him, whose clothing looked as if it had seen better days. The sleeves of his jacket were frayed at the cuffs, and it needed a good cleaning. His appearance was in stark contrast to Mr. Stryker's, who was clad in an expensive-looking tweed sports jacket and brown corduroy slacks.

Nancy looked at the menu, but she was distracted by Mr. Stryker's voice. Although she couldn't hear all he said, she did hear Mr. Stryker mention something about a shining stream. And a cave. And the name of Hank Tolchinsky. His voice got angrier as he spoke.

Interesting, Nancy thought. Just as she put her menu down to listen more closely, Mr. Stryker stood up.

As he walked past Nancy's booth he stared at her. Was she imagining it, or did he look alarmed to see her?

Nancy called out his name, but Mr. Stryker kept moving and was soon out the door. The man he'd been talking to remained in the booth, scowling as he finished his cup of coffee.

George, who had noticed Mr. Stryker's abrupt departure, too, gave Nancy a puzzled look.

Bess, glancing up from her menu, saw her friends' faces and asked them what was the matter.

Nancy, leaning over the table, spoke softly to Bess and George, repeating what she had heard Mr. Stryker say.

George's eyebrows rose as she listened. "Who's that man?" she asked quietly, her eyes darting to the booth behind them.

Nancy shrugged. "I don't know," she said, just as he rose and shambled out of the shop.

The waitress approached and took their order. After she'd finished writing, Nancy spoke up.

"Do you know who that was talking to John Stryker?"

"That's Ralph Bremer," the waitress replied, sniffing as she mentioned his name. "He owns the hardware store down the street, and I wish he'd keep it up better. It's becoming an eyesore." She turned on her heel and headed toward the kitchen.

"What do you think it means?" George asked, as they waited for their lunch to arrive.

"Maybe something," Nancy said. "Or maybe nothing. Let's file it away. It may come in handy later."

The girls ate their lunch, had their pie— Nancy and George without whipped cream and Bess with—and then decided to finish window-shopping before heading back to Aunt Elizabeth's.

They paid for their lunch, leaving a tip for the waitress, and then left the coffee shop.

Strolling down Main Street, they came across a toy store. The front window was filled with stuffed animals, displayed in a zoo setting. Bess was admiring an orangutan hanging from an artificial tree when Nancy saw something that made her catch her breath.

"Look!" she said, pointing. There, hanging by an invisible string from the ceiling of the display window, was a stuffed bat just like the one that had been left hanging on Aunt Elizabeth's porch.

"It's exactly the same!" George exclaimed.

"Let's go in," Bess said. "Maybe whoever bought Aunt Elizabeth's bat bought it here."

"That's just what I was thinking." Nancy pushed open the door and the three of them went into the store.

Behind the counter stood a brown-haired woman dressed in a bright green dress, chatting with a customer holding a stuffed bear.

Nancy went up to the counter.

The salesclerk turned to her. "May I help you with something?"

"That bat in the window," Nancy said. "Has anyone bought one of those recently?"

The clerk eyed her skeptically. "Why do you want to know?"

Nancy thought quickly. "I'd like to buy one for a friend. She admired it in the window the other day. But I don't want to buy it if she already has."

"I suppose I could look at my sales slips," the clerk said, pulling out the cash register drawer.

"But unless your friend charged it, there's no way of telling."

Nancy's heart sank. How likely would it be that Sarah would use a charge card?

"I do remember a girl about your age bought it," the clerk said, leafing through the slips. "But I don't recall who exactly. What was your friend's name?"

Nancy was trying to decide whether or not to give her Sarah's name when the door to the store opened and a young woman with two children entered. The children clamored over a group of stuffed monkeys on one of the shelves and began pulling them off excitedly.

The clerk immediately rushed to the shelves. "Wait a second!" she cried. "Let's take them down one at a time."

Nancy discreetly pulled the sales slips over to her.

"Nancy!" Bess exclaimed. "Do you have to be so sneaky?"

"Fairport is a small town," Nancy whispered, leafing through the sales slips furiously. "I don't want it to get around that we're suspicious of Sarah."

The clerk was distracted enough not to notice Nancy's search. Before long, Nancy found a slip that answered her question. It didn't have

62

Sarah's name on it. But it did have her mother's and a charge card number.

The clerk had said someone Nancy's age had bought the bat. It must have been Sarah, with her mother. But was that enough to prove the girl's guilt?

7

A Splash in the Dark

Nancy waved goodbye to the clerk, who was still busy with the children. When Nancy and her friends left the store, she told them what she'd discovered.

"So Sarah did buy it," George said, her eyes lighting up.

"But that doesn't prove she's the one who left it on the porch, does it?" Bess asked.

"Exactly," Nancy said. "Someone else could have bought one as well. With cash," she added.

"Let's go back to Aunt Elizabeth's," George said. "And tell her all about it."

They returned to the car. Nancy could see that Mr. Bremer was back in his hardware store, sitting at a counter and gazing out the window. He stared at them while she and her friends got into the car. Was it only boredom, Nancy wondered, or was there something else behind his stare?

On the way back to Aunt Elizabeth's, they talked about Sarah.

"Much as I have sympathy for Sarah's feelings," Nancy said, "if she's the one who's done all these things, I think she's gone too far."

"Aunt Elizabeth is putting up a good front," George replied. "But I think she's frightened."

"I would be too," Nancy said. "Why can't Sarah look at this more reasonably?"

"She's scared, I guess," Bess said. "And she's hurting. That can make people do things they wouldn't ordinarily do."

They pulled up at Aunt Elizabeth's. She was out front, potting a flat of petunias in a terra-cotta planter.

"Something's bothering you, I can tell," she said, straightening up to greet them when they got out of the car. "Your faces look troubled. Come inside and tell me what's on your minds."

In the parlor Nancy told her about what they had discovered at the toy shop.

"That would seem to implicate Sarah, wouldn't it?" Aunt Elizabeth said with a sigh.

"Yes," Nancy agreed. "But there's more." Briefly, she told her about the conversation she'd overheard between John Stryker and Ralph

Bremer. "Mr. Stryker seemed very angry," Nancy said.

"I wouldn't describe Ralph Bremer as one of Fairport's most upstanding citizens," Aunt Elizabeth observed. "That store of his has been going downhill so rapidly. I think he has money problems. But what would he be talking to John Stryker about? They've never been friendly."

Was this another piece of the puzzle? Nancy wondered. Or something unrelated?

Before she could say more, the phone rang. Aunt Elizabeth answered it, and then handed it over to Nancy. "It's Jessie," she said. "She wants to talk to you."

Nancy took the phone from Aunt Elizabeth, and said hello to Jessie.

"I have to tell you about something odd I saw today," Jessie said. "It may mean something, it may not."

"Tell me," Nancy said. "We were just sitting here trying to sort things out."

"Well," Jessie said, "I was on my way into town this morning, driving along Old Fairport Road. I was just about to go over that little bridge when I saw Sarah."

"Was she on the bridge?" Nancy asked.

"No," Jessie said. "She was walking away from it. And here's the weird part. I think she recognized me in the car. And as soon as she saw me, she turned and ran away. She disappeared into the woods."

"What could she have been doing out there?" Nancy asked.

"I don't know," Jessie replied. "Maybe she's looking for the cave."

"But why would she want to find it?" Nancy asked. "After all, it's the cave that will prove the trees can't be taken down. It's not in her interest to find the cave."

"But it would be in her interest to hide it, wouldn't it?" Jessie said. "We know the cave isn't easily found. Professor Noble's been looking for it for a while. The opening to it must be hard to see. If she found it, she could cover it up even more so we'd never find it."

"Hmm," Nancy said. "You have a point." Briefly, Nancy told Jessie about what they had discovered at the toy shop. And then she mentioned running into John Stryker and Ralph Bremer at the coffee shop.

"Something's going on here," Jessie said. "And I hope we figure it out soon. Professor Noble and I are going out this afternoon to look for the cave. If we don't find it today, we're going to look again tomorrow," Jessie said. "Would you like to come?"

"I'd love to," Nancy said.

"I'll call you tomorrow," Jessie said, and hung up.

Nancy was just about to return to the parlor when the phone rang again.

"Porter residence," Nancy said when she picked it up.

"Is Mrs. Porter there?" asked a high-pitched and muffled voice. Nancy suspected this was the caller who had threatened Aunt Elizabeth the other night. But was the caller a woman or a man? She couldn't tell.

"No, she isn't," Nancy said. She hoped the caller would stay on the line. The longer she heard the voice, the more she'd have to work with in trying to figure out who it could be.

"Tell her she'd better watch her back because I'm watching her!" The caller hung up.

Ashen-faced, Nancy returned to her friends in the parlor.

"Another nasty call?" Aunt Elizabeth asked.

Nancy nodded. "And Jessie told me she saw Sarah near the bridge on Old Fairport Road today, looking suspicious. I think a visit to the Connor house is in order after dinner, don't you?" Nancy asked her friends.

*   *   *

"Should I come along?" Aunt Elizabeth asked after dinner as Nancy, Bess, and George got ready to leave.

"I don't know if it would do any good for you to confront Sarah," Nancy told her. "She'd be even more reluctant to admit she's doing it if you were there, don't you think?"

Aunt Elizabeth nodded. "You're right. If you could settle this by simply talking to her and explaining how unnecessary it is, perhaps that would be best."

"And we'll keep the police out of it for now?" Nancy asked.

"If she confesses, then we can just forget about it," Aunt Elizabeth said. "If she doesn't, then we'll talk to them."

"I'm going to stay with Aunt E.," George said as the girls went into the vestibule to get their jackets. "I don't want to leave her alone."

"That's a good idea," Nancy said. "Besides, Bess and I aren't related to your aunt. Sarah might be more willing to confide in us."

As she and Bess headed out on Old Fairport Road, Nancy wondered what they would find when they got to Sarah's house. Would Sarah be willing to talk? Or would she still be angry and confrontational?

As she took a turn slowly, Nancy glanced in the

69

rearview mirror. Was she imagining it, or did she see the dark outline of a car behind them, just as she had last night?

"Bess, look back," she said. "Do you see anything?"

Bess turned and looked. "No," she said.

The road straightened and Nancy continued to drive slowly. As she went around a curve, she thought she heard a car engine.

"Look again," she told Bess. "I hear someone behind us. I think we're being followed again."

"But we were in Aunt Elizabeth's car last night when we were being followed," Bess reminded her. "They were after her. Why would anyone be after us?"

"I don't know," Nancy said. "But keep looking back."

As she took another sharp turn, Nancy looked in the rearview mirror. Now she could see it clearly. "Look!" she cried.

"You're right!" Bess exclaimed.

Nancy slowed down even further. The car caught up and tailgated them, the front end not more than a couple of inches away from her rear bumper. Why would the driver follow so closely? And how could someone drive so expertly without headlights?

"Nancy, watch out!" Bess cried.

The dark car hit the rear bumper and pushed Nancy's car far to the right. Nancy tried to keep on the road, but it was impossible. Her car hit the wooden rail of the bridge and plowed over the edge, heading straight for the water.

8

A Cry of Innocence

Bess screamed as the car pitched headfirst into the water. The car hit bottom with a sickening thud.

"Bess, are you all right?" Nancy cried.

Bess's voice quavered in the darkness. "Yes, I think so."

Their seat belts held Nancy and Bess in place even though the car was pitched forward at a steep angle. Water came up to the bottom half of the windshield.

"I think we're going to have to climb into the back to get out," Nancy said to Bess.

The engine was still running. Nancy turned it off, undid her seat belt, and began to clamber back. Bess followed.

Nancy threw open the back door and saw that the only way to get out was to jump.

"Here goes," she cried, and jumped.

When her feet hit the bottom of the stream, the water came up to her knees. Bess followed quickly, squealing as she hit the cold water.

In pitch-blackness, Nancy and Bess slogged to the side of the stream, then scrambled up the bank to the side of the road.

"Were you able to see the make of the car?" Bess asked Nancy as they stood dripping and hoping to see the comforting headlights of a car that could bring help.

"I think so," Nancy said. "From the shape of its rear end I could see it was a Saab. I wish I could have seen the license plate."

"Well, at least we have the model," Bess said. "We're going to the police, aren't we?"

"We have to," Nancy said. "This is beyond childish pranks. We could have been killed."

"Don't remind me," Bess said with a shiver.

They trembled in the breeze of the dark spring night. An owl hooted somewhere in the nearby woods. How long would they have to wait? Nancy wondered.

Finally, she saw a pair of headlights round the curve. Nancy waved and the car stopped.

A middle-aged woman with frosted blond hair rolled down her window. "Are you in trouble?" she asked.

She looked familiar, Nancy thought, guessing that she'd probably seen her at the town meeting. Nancy quickly explained their situation, making it sound like an accident.

"Hop in. I'll take you back to my house and call a tow truck." The woman opened the back door for Nancy and Bess.

"Could you take us to Elizabeth Porter's house instead?" Nancy asked, and gave her the address. "That's where we're staying."

"I thought you looked familiar," the woman said as she turned her car around. "You're friends of Elizabeth's niece, aren't you?"

Nancy nodded, shivering next to her.

"I'm Janet Ellsworth. I'm a friend of Elizabeth's." She sighed. "I'm afraid Elizabeth has gotten herself into the thick of things with this bat project," she said.

"You're not on the side of the bats?" Nancy asked.

"No, this road is dangerous. What just happened to you is a good example of that. It should be widened, bats or not."

Nancy wondered what Mrs. Ellsworth would think if she knew how dangerous the road really was.

Mrs. Ellsworth went on. "If our town manager would pay a little more attention to the town budget than his regattas, we'd be in much better shape."

"His regattas?" Nancy asked. She hadn't heard anything about this before.

"Oh, I suppose you don't know. John's quite the sailor. I have a friend who works at Town Hall, and she says he spent a couple of weeks this winter sailing around the Caribbean when he should have been back here taking care of business."

She pulled into Aunt Elizabeth's driveway. Nancy filed away what Mrs. Ellsworth had said for later reference, thanked her for the ride, and hopped out of the car with Bess.

Aunt Elizabeth and George looked alarmed when they saw the state of Nancy's and Bess's clothing. When Nancy explained what had happened, Mrs. Porter frowned.

"I'll call Gerri Spinetti," she said, walking to the phone. "This is the last straw."

While Aunt Elizabeth made her call to the police, Nancy and Bess ran upstairs to change. When they returned, George offered to drive them to the police station.

"Officer Spinetti says she thinks she may be able to track down the owner of that car," Aunt Elizabeth told Nancy.

"Let's go then," Nancy said, eager to solve at least one part of the mystery. She grabbed a flashlight lying on the table in the vestibule. It would be good to have it later while she waited for the tow truck.

George dropped them off in front of the police station. "Much as I'd like to solve this mystery with you, I'm going to have to go back to Aunt E.'s," George said. "I can't leave her alone. Not after this. Aunt E. said Officer Spinetti would drive you home when you're done. Good luck!"

When they entered the building, Nancy found the bright lights of the police station comforting after what she and Bess had been through. A plump, dark-haired woman smiled as she rose from her desk to greet them.

Her smile turned to a frown, however, when Nancy told her what had happened.

"They had no lights on?" she asked.

Nancy nodded. "And it's not the first time we've seen that car." She went on to tell Officer Spinetti about what had happened the night before.

"Can you tell me the make of the car? Or the color?" she asked.

"It was a Saab," Nancy said. "It looked black when my headlights shined on it briefly."

"We can run a search on the make and color of the car and see what happens," Officer Spinetti said. "It may lead to nothing, but then again, there can't be that many Saabs in Fairport."

Nancy and Bess sat next to her on metal chairs

as she logged on to her computer and tapped the information Nancy had given her into the vehicle database.

The computer whirred. A list of names popped up on the screen.

Officer Spinetti turned the screen toward Nancy. "There are only a few people with that car," she noted. "Anybody sound familiar?" Her finger ran down the list and stopped at the last name.

"Sarah Connor," she said. "No need to worry there."

Nancy turned to Officer Spinetti. "There's a great deal to worry about there," she said. "We're going to need your help.

It didn't take Nancy long to tell Officer Spinetti of her suspicions about Sarah. She explained the threatening phone calls, the stuffed bat they'd found hanging from Aunt Elizabeth's porch rafter, and the fact that Sarah had purchased a bat exactly like it from a local toy store.

"I know Margaret Connor well," Officer Spinetti said, "and I'm sure she'd want to know if Sarah was doing anything dangerous. I don't think it's out of line to pay her and Sarah a visit tonight." She turned off her computer. "Maybe we can get this cleared up."

"What about my car?" Nancy asked. "It's still sitting in the stream."

"We'll call a tow truck after we visit the

Connors," Gerri Spinetti said. "I don't think it will take long."

Nancy and Bess climbed into Officer Spinetti's police car. On the way to the Connors, Nancy told her more about the telephone threats Aunt Elizabeth had been receiving.

"Why didn't she call me when this first started happening?" Officer Spinetti asked. "You could have been badly hurt."

"She thought they were just pranks," Nancy explained. "She was hoping that if it was Sarah, she'd stop."

"Well, obviously if it's her, she hasn't," said the officer. "But she will put an end to this by the time I get through with her. I have a real soft spot for Elizabeth Porter," she said, "and not much patience for anyone who's annoying her."

Nancy thought for a moment before speaking. "If you don't mind, could I speak to Sarah first? She might be more willing to talk to someone her own age."

Wearing a surprised expression, Officer Spinetti turned and looked at Nancy. "You sound like you know what you're talking about," she said.

"Nancy's a detective," Bess spoke up. "She solves mysteries."

Officer Spinetti gave Nancy a long look. "Well, let's hope you can solve this one."

When they pulled into the Connor driveway,

Nancy saw a black Saab parked in front of the garage.

Officer Spinetti parked the police car, and they got out. "That's the car!" Bess whispered as they approached the front door of the house.

"Maybe," Nancy whispered back. As they passed the Saab, she put her hand on the hood. It was still warm, proof that the car had recently been used.

Officer Spinetti knocked on the door. When Mrs. Connor opened it and saw who was there, she looked surprised.

"Is something wrong?" she asked. She motioned the officer and the girls into the foyer.

"I'm afraid there is," Officer Spinetti said. She explained what had happened to Nancy and Bess.

Mrs. Connor's eyes widened. "How awful!" she exclaimed. "But what does it have to do with us?"

Officer Spinetti looked at Nancy. This was her cue to begin.

"The car that ran us off the road was a Saab just like the one out front," Nancy said.

Mrs. Connor looked confused. "But we've been here all night," she said. "Sarah's been up in her room and I've been downstairs. You don't think . . ."

"We don't know what to think," Nancy said

gently. She went on to tell Mrs. Connor about the threatening phone calls and the stuffed bat. "We know Sarah's been very upset," Nancy concluded. "And sometimes when people are upset they do foolish things."

Sarah appeared at the top of the stairs. "What is it, Mother?" she asked. Then she saw Nancy and Bess. "Oh, it's you."

Sarah came down slowly. Nancy could see her eyes were red. She must have been crying.

Her mother turned to her. "Officer Spinetti is here to ask us about our car. It seems a car just like it ran these two girls off the road about an hour ago."

Sarah looked at Nancy and Bess, and then at Officer Spinetti. "So?" she said.

Nancy stepped in. "Sarah, where have you been this evening?"

Sarah gave her a belligerent look. "In my room—reading."

Nancy knew she had been doing more than reading, from the looks of her eyes. "You haven't taken the car out?"

"No," Sarah replied, frowning. She turned to her mother. "Did you see me go out?" she asked sarcastically.

"No, and I've told Officer Spinetti that you've been here all evening."

"Then why is the hood of your car warm?" Bess burst out.

"I don't know. I keep the keys in the ignition, you know, just like everyone else in Fairport," she said sullenly. "Maybe someone borrowed it."

Nancy thought that wasn't likely. But if Sarah had been out, wouldn't her mother have known? Or was Mrs. Connor covering up for Sarah?

Nancy raised an eyebrow. Then she asked, "Sarah, do you have any stuffed animals?"

"Of course I do. Don't you?"

Nancy smiled. "Do you have a stuffed bat?"

For a moment Sarah looked angry. Then she recovered. "As a matter of fact, I do. I saw it the other day at a toy store on the green, and I just had to have it. It seemed fitting somehow," she said with a bitter laugh.

"Can I see it?" Nancy asked.

Sarah gave Nancy a long look. Then she looked at Officer Spinetti and must have realized that Nancy had the police officer's backing. Wordlessly, she went back up the stairs.

The group stood nervously in the hall, waiting for Sarah to return.

When she did, her face was the picture of confusion. "It's not there," she said, rubbing her forehead. "It's gone."

Nancy looked at Bess. Now Bess raised her eyebrows.

"I put it on my dresser the other morning," Sarah said. "I remember that." She began to cry.

Nancy went over to Sarah and put an arm around her shoulder. "Someone has been threatening Mrs. Porter. We've been getting phone calls, and the other night someone left a stuffed bat just like yours on her porch with a death threat attached to it. If it's you who's been doing these things, we can understand it's out of unhappiness."

Sarah threw off Nancy's arm. "How could you think such a thing!" She looked at her mother, her eyes wide with fright, and back to Nancy. "Do you really think I ran you off the road? After what happened to my brother?"

"Sarah, your mother said you were here all night," Nancy said. "We're going to accept that. We're sorry we disturbed you, and we'll be on our way now."

Nancy motioned to Bess and Officer Spinetti to accompany her out the door.

"Well done," Officer Spinetti said to Nancy when the door had closed behind them.

"But she denied everything," Bess said.

Nancy smiled. "Yes, she did. And maybe that's the truth. But if it isn't, at least she's been warned that we're onto her."

"Maybe those threats will finally stop now,"

Officer Spinetti said as they got into her car. "I'll take you back to Mrs. Porter's."

"If you don't mind," Nancy said, "would you call a tow truck on your radio and drop me off at my car?"

Officer Spinetti called a towing company, and the driver promised to get there as soon as possible. Then she drove Nancy back to the site of the accident.

"Bess, go on back to Aunt E.'s," Nancy said as she got out of the car.

"Is that a good idea?" Bess asked. "It's awfully dark."

"The tow truck will be here soon," Nancy said. "I'm not afraid to wait in the dark. And I have a flashlight." She pulled it out of her jeans pocket.

"Are you sure?" Officer Spinetti asked.

"Positive," Nancy replied.

Officer Spinetti and Bess drove off, leaving Nancy on the side of the road. The night was clear and chilly, with a crescent moon just beginning to rise above the trees.

Nancy shined her flashlight on the bridge, picking out the railing that had given way as the car went over. Then she saw something that piqued her curiosity.

She strode to the bridge to get a closer look. In the beam of the flashlight she saw that the break in the railing wasn't splintered as she'd expected it to be from the impact of the car. In fact, as she examined it more closely, she could see it had been sawed apart.

She realized, with a start, that the only reason why the railing had given way when her car hit it was because it had been tampered with.

She and Bess had ended up in the stream because someone had wanted them there.

But who?

9

The Search Is On!

When the tow truck arrived, Nancy greeted the young man who drove it and pointed out the car in the stream below.

"My name's Fred," he said. "I'll go down and take a look at it.

As he scrambled down the bank and waded into the water, Nancy heard a rustling in the woods behind her. When she turned she saw a man in dark clothes, standing silently. It was Mr. Tolchinsky.

"Had an accident?" he said. He stepped onto the road and approached her.

"Yes," Nancy said. "My car went off the bridge."

"I heard the tow truck arrive back at the house," he said, "and came out to see what was going on."

"Didn't you hear us when we crashed?" Nancy

85

asked. "That would have made a much louder noise."

"I've been listening to music," Mr. Tolchinsky said. "Are you all right?"

"I'm fine," Nancy said.

"Good," Mr. Tolchinsky said.

Should she tell him she knew the bridge had been tampered with? But he might have been the one who tampered with it, Nancy figured. She didn't have a chance to decide. In the next instant, Mr. Tolchinsky turned on his heel and disappeared into the woods.

It didn't take Fred long to hook the car up to the winch on the back of the truck and tow it out.

When the car was out of the creek, he hopped out of the truck and went around to see if there was any damage.

"Looks okay," he said. "I'd let it dry out before you try to start it, though," he advised.

"I don't think I'll be doing any more driving tonight," Nancy said with a laugh.

"Hop in," Fred said. "I'll take you home."

Nancy gave him directions to Aunt Elizabeth's house. It wasn't long before he turned into her driveway.

"Here you are," he said cheerfully.

Nancy hopped out of the truck, thanked him, and went into the house. Her friends were in the parlor drinking hot cocoa with Aunt Elizabeth.

"Nancy, you look troubled," George said.

Nancy sank into an easy chair. "I found out someone tampered with the bridge."

"What!" Bess exclaimed.

"Someone sawed off the railing," Nancy replied. "We never would have gone into the stream otherwise."

"So someone deliberately forced you off the bridge," George said, looking alarmed. "Someone planned it."

"Exactly," Nancy said. "And Mr. Tolchinsky showed up while Fred, the tow truck operator, pulled the car out. He said he'd heard the truck approaching. When I told him I was fine, he walked off."

"Do you think he was the one who did that to the railing?" Aunt Elizabeth asked.

"I don't know," Nancy said. "Jessie told me she saw Sarah around there this afternoon."

"It could be either one of them," George said.

"Except we know it was Sarah's car that pushed us off," Nancy reminded them. "Or someone driving Sarah's car."

George perked right up. "I didn't think of that! Do you think Tolchinsky could have taken her car and used it to throw us off the track?"

Nancy shrugged. "There's a lot more we need to know," she said.

"What I want to know," Aunt Elizabeth said,

"is why someone ran your car off the road, Nancy. Why would anyone be after you?"

"Someone must know Nancy is trying to find out who's threatening you, Aunt E.," George said. "So now Nancy's a target, too."

The group was silent for a moment, and then Aunt Elizabeth spoke up. "Nancy, Professor Noble called just a couple of minutes ago and said he and Jessie didn't find the cave today. He'd like you to help him look for it tomorrow. He'll pick you up in the afternoon."

"That means a visit to Mr. Tolchinsky as well," Nancy said firmly. "We've got to get to the bottom of this. And quickly."

With that, they went upstairs to bed. Tomorrow, after the crafts fair, they'd look for the cave. There wasn't much time to find it—or whoever was threatening Nancy and Aunt Elizabeth.

When Nancy, Bess, and George arrived at the crafts fair late the next morning, the activities were in full swing. Colorful booths lined the sidewalks of the green, offering everything from decorative flowerpots to handcrafted jewelry.

As Nancy stood at one booth, purchasing a beautiful handwoven shawl she knew would be perfect for Hannah, she heard her name being called.

It was Jessie. "Mrs. Porter told me you'd be

here," she said. "I'm glad I found you. Are you coming with the professor and me this afternoon?"

Nancy nodded. "Did she tell you what happened last night?"

"Yes, she did. It's very peculiar," Jessie said. "I have to tell you something that's even more peculiar."

"Tell me," Nancy said. Would it be the clue that made the mystery make sense? Or just another piece to a puzzle that wasn't falling into place yet?

"I ran into Chuck Danzig the other day," Jessie began. "Remember him? He's the man from the state fish and game agency who developed the habitat conservation plan for the town."

"Right," Nancy said. "I remember him. He spoke at the town meeting."

"He told me something odd," Jessie said. "He said that when he came to the Town Hall to get the surveyor's map for the site, Mr. Stryker told him he only had a day to complete his habitat report. And when Chuck told Mr. Stryker it usually took him several days to do a proper assessment, Mr. Stryker said he was sorry, but he could only have one day, and that was that."

"Why would it matter to Mr. Stryker?" Nancy asked.

"Exactly," Jessie said. "And the really weird thing is that Mr. Stryker insisted on accompanying Chuck to the site, and he stayed with him the whole time. Chuck said he felt as if Mr. Stryker kept leading him away from certain areas, although it was done in such a subtle way that he couldn't protest."

Nancy thought about this for a while. It certainly was odd. But how did it fit in?

"Look who's here." Jessie muttered under her breath, giving Nancy a poke with her elbow.

Nancy looked where Jessie pointed. At the edge of the green Mr. Stryker was talking to Mr. Bremer. It was an angry conversation, from the look on Mr. Stryker's face.

Mr. Stryker shouted some last words at Mr. Bremer, turned on his heel, and stalked away.

"What do you think that was all about?" Jessie asked.

"I don't know," Nancy replied. "But as they say in the movies—the plot is definitely thickening!"

Professor Noble and Jessie arrived at the Porters' later that afternoon. Nancy and her friends piled into his car and they headed off on Old Fairport Road.

"I'm going to park in a friend's driveway," Professor Noble told them, "and then we'll hike from there. I'd rather not run into Tolchinsky if it's at all possible."

"I wouldn't mind running into him," Nancy said. She told him about what had happened the previous night.

"So now the suspicion is on Mr. Tolchinsky?" Professor Noble asked.

Nancy nodded. "After all, the car was run off the road near his house."

Professor Noble thought for a moment. "You know, the suspects are starting to mount up. There's Sarah and Tolchinsky. And after what Jessie has told me about her conversation with Chuck, I'm beginning to wonder if Stryker might not be involved in some way."

"Aunt Elizabeth thinks it's odd how easily he caved in to the environmentalists' point of view," George said.

"But when I saw him the other day," Professor Noble said, "he tried to convince me that it wasn't worth looking for the cave. He said he thought we had a pretty strong case as it was."

"You'd think if he was in favor of the bats, he'd want you to find the cave, wouldn't you?" Nancy asked.

"My thoughts exactly," Professor Noble said. "It looks as though quite a few Fairporters are behaving suspiciously."

He pulled into a driveway that was well hidden

from the road by a stand of trees. When they got out of the car, Professor Noble reminded the girls to walk quietly and disturb the woods as little as possible. They made their way along the side of the road until they reached the grove of oaks.

"I've searched this area thoroughly," Professor Noble said as they stood beneath the oaks, "and I haven't been able to find anything. But I know if these bats are here, a cave has to be nearby."

"Wouldn't a cave be part of a rock formation above the ground?" Nancy asked.

Professor Noble shook his head. "Not necessarily. It could be underground. That's what makes finding it so difficult."

"I have one question," Bess said. "Will there be bats in the cave? I hate to admit it, but I'm a little scared of bats."

Professor Noble laughed softly. "I understand your fear, Bess. Not to worry. Most of them will have left the cave because it's spring. There may still be a few there, but not enough to cause you any trouble."

"Well, shall we break up and search in different directions?" Nancy asked, eager to begin the hunt.

"I think you girls should go in teams," Professor Noble said. "With what's been going on around here, I think it's best you don't wander alone. I know the woods pretty well, so I'll be okay by myself."

The girls agreed and teamed up: Nancy with Jessie, and Bess with George.

"If you find anything, come back here. Don't yell out," Professor Noble said. "We want to keep our whereabouts a secret for now."

Nancy and Jessie headed out together. "If you were a cave, where would you be?" Jessie asked with a laugh.

"I think I would be underground, since Professor Noble hasn't found one aboveground," Nancy said.

"That makes a lot of sense," Jessie said.

The two girls walked through the woods and soon came to a creek.

"This must be the stream my car went into," Nancy remarked. A stray sunbeam broke through the foliage and sparkled on the water. The sight brought to mind a phrase she'd recently heard. "The shining stream," she whispered.

"The shining stream. What's that?" Jessie asked.

"Something I overheard Mr. Stryker talking about with Mr. Bremer. It was somehow connected with Mr. Tolchinsky as well," Nancy told her.

They walked along the banks of the stream,

their eyes roaming the ground for anything unusual.

"Look at that!" Nancy pointed to a fallen tree. Just behind it, almost obscured by a branch, was a depression in the earth.

Nancy ran to it with Jessie right behind her. Leaves filled the depression. Scooping them out by the handful, Nancy revealed an opening into the ground. Could this be the cave?

"I think you've found it," Jessie said, keeping her excited voice a whisper.

Together they hastily scooped out more of the leaves to clear the opening further. When they finally uncovered it, they saw it was as wide as a man's shoulders.

"There's cold air coming out," Jessie said, excited. "This has to be it!"

"Should we go back?" Nancy asked.

Jessie reached for her belt and removed a small flashlight. "Not until we know for sure," she said. "I'm going in."

"Not alone, you're not," Nancy said. "Who knows what's inside?"

"All right," Jessie said. "But I'll go in first and lead the way."

She went in feetfirst. Nancy waited at the opening until she heard Jessie's feet drop onto solid ground.

"It's a bit of jump, but you can make it," Jessie called up.

Then Nancy heard her scream.

Nancy immediately dropped down into the hole. She slid a bit and staggered when she landed on what felt like wet rock beneath her feet.

The cave was black, except for the beam of Jessie's flashlight, roaming skittishly across the walls of the cave.

"What is it?" Nancy asked anxiously.

"Look!" Jessie said. She focused the beam on the bottom of the cave.

The floor of the cave was littered with what at first looked like dried leaves. But on closer examination, Nancy saw that they weren't leaves at all. They were bats. Hundreds of them. And they were all dead.

10

A Veil of Secrecy Lifts

The flashlight shook in Jessie's hand, causing the beam to flit across the floor. Nancy took the flashlight from Jessie and shined it around the cave.

It was small, with a low ceiling. An opening in the wall to her right, big enough for a body to squeeze through, indicated that the cave went on farther. Nancy shined the beam on something leaning against the wall. "What's that?" she exclaimed.

Jessie walked over to it. "It's a shovel. Ugh!" she cried out, and dropped it. Making a face, she pulled off her gloves.

"What's wrong?" Nancy asked.

Jessie nudged the shovel with her foot. "Someone must have used this to kill the bats." She examined her gloves and put them back on.

Nancy, who was also wearing gloves, picked up the shovel and shined the flashlight on the spade. Blood and bits of fur were stuck to the metal.

She grimaced and dropped it. "I wonder if we could trace it to its owner," she said. "We'll have to take it aboveground. Maybe it has fingerprints, though I don't think they'll do us much good."

"I've heard of this kind of slaughter," Jessie said, her voice shaking, "but I never thought I'd see it, not here in Fairport. Whoever did this must not know they can be arrested for killing an endangered species. It's a federal crime."

"Either they don't know or they don't care," Nancy said. "This was a violent act against innocent animals."

Jessie shuddered. "Let's get out of here."

Nancy gave Jessie a boost so she could grab the edges of the cave opening and scramble out.

"Here's the shovel," Nancy called, and hoisted it up to Jessie's waiting hand.

Nancy heard the handle scrape against the cave opening as Jessie lifted out the shovel.

"Okay, you're next," Jessie said. Nancy grabbed her hand. Jessie pulled her up until she could squirm out.

It felt strange to be back aboveground again, in the bright sun and fresh air. Nancy took the shovel, and she and Jessie walked quietly back to where they had begun their search. Nancy leaned the shovel against a tree trunk, and they collapsed on the ground under one of the oaks.

"Do you think whoever did this could be the same person who's been threatening Aunt Elizabeth?" Nancy asked Jessie.

"I don't know," Jessie said. "I've heard stories about people killing bats just for the fun of it, if you can believe that."

"But the notes and the phone calls Aunt Elizabeth's been getting have all hinted at violence and death," Nancy reminded her. "And they've all been connected to the bats. What better way to resolve the situation than to kill off the bats?"

Nancy was about to ask whether the bats were still hibernating when she heard footsteps crunching on leaves. A moment later Professor Noble came into the clearing.

"Any luck?" he asked.

"We found the cave," Jessie said.

"Wonderful!" Professor Noble exclaimed. "We'll have to—"

"But it was filled with dead bats," Jessie said, interrupting him.

He stopped in his tracks. "Dead?"

Jessie pointed to the shovel. "There's the murder weapon."

"I've seen this kind of senseless act before,"

Professor Noble said. "Usually it's teenagers trying to be cool."

"In this case," Nancy said, "I don't think so."

"I agree with you," Professor Noble said. He walked over to the shovel.

"Don't handle it without gloves, please," Nancy said.

Professor Noble put on a pair of gloves, then picked up the shovel and hefted it. "Thank goodness most of the bats were already out of the cave after their winter hibernation. A stunt like this can kill off a whole colony."

Nancy saw something on the handle of the shovel that she hadn't noticed in the darkness of the cave. It looked like a price tag. She walked over to get a closer look.

"Fairport Hardware," she said as she scrutinized the tag.

"That's Mr. Bremer's store," Jessie noted.

"Interesting," Nancy said. "I've seen him and Mr. Stryker together twice in the past couple of days. They were arguing both times."

"But it doesn't necessarily mean anything," Professor Noble reminded her. "Anyone could have bought this shovel. Like Hank Tolchinsky, for instance."

"He made it pretty clear he hates bats, didn't he?" Nancy said.

"Killing them off would certainly end his problems," Professor Noble said.

Nancy heard rustling in the woods. Bess and George entered the clearing. Bess was leaning on George's shoulder, limping.

"I twisted my ankle!" she moaned. "And it hurts."

Nancy rushed to her friend. Together, she and George helped Bess over to a rock under a tree, where she sat down. Nancy looked at her ankle. It was bruised and swollen. "I hope it's not broken," she said.

Professor Noble and Jessie gathered around Bess. "Do you think you can make it to the car?" Professor Noble asked.

Bess, close to tears, shook her head. "I've gone about as far as I can," she said.

"If it's broken, we don't want Bess to put any more strain on it," Nancy said.

"No, we wouldn't want that, now, would we?" a sarcastic voice bellowed out behind them.

Nancy turned around and saw Hank Tolchinsky at the edge of the clearing, glowering at them.

"My friend has hurt her ankle," Nancy said, angry at his sarcasm. "She's in a lot of pain. Can't you have some sympathy?"

"I usually don't waste my sympathy on trespassers."

"And I suppose you don't waste it on bats, either, do you?" Jessie blurted out.

"I think I've made that clear," Mr. Tolchinsky replied. "Were you looking for your long-lost cave?"

"Yes, we were, and we found it," Nancy said. "We also found something else."

Mr. Tolchinsky raised his eyebrows. "Would you care to tell me about it?" he asked.

"The cave was filled with dead bats," Nancy replied. She watched his reaction closely.

"You're looking at me as if I had something to do with it," Mr. Tolchinsky said, his voice cold and low. "I didn't."

"Do you expect us to believe you?" Professor Noble asked. "Is this your shovel?"

Mr. Tolchinsky turned to him. "No, it's not. Whether you believe me or not, I'm telling the truth. I don't know why wanting to maintain my privacy makes me so suspect in Fairport," he said. "It's not a crime to want to be left alone."

Was that all Mr. Tolchinsky wanted? Nancy wondered. Or was he just a good actor?

"Look," she said, "our friend is hurt. We need to call an ambulance and get her to the hospital. Since your house is nearby, could we use your phone?"

Nancy saw George give her a quick, questioning look. She knew George was concerned for her safety. There was no way to tell her that she was using this opportunity to angle her way into Mr. Tolchinsky's house, but she knew George would trust her judgment.

Mr. Tolchinsky shifted his feet.

"I know you won't turn down a reasonable request," Nancy said, hoping to bring him around. She had to get into that house!

Mr. Tolchinsky gave her a long look. "I'll call an ambulance for you," he said. "Would that be good enough?"

Nancy forced herself to smile. "That's very generous," she said, thinking quickly, "but I also need to call Mrs. Porter. She'll be worried because we're not back yet."

Mr. Tolchinsky shrugged his shoulders in exasperation. "All right," he finally said. "Come along."

Nancy began to follow him out of the clearing, when he stopped and turned to her friends.

"Don't worry," he said. "She's safe. My bark is much worse than my bite."

"We'll be waiting right here," Professor Noble said, "for her return."

Nancy followed Mr. Tolchinsky deep into the woods. She wondered about his remark. Was he sincere? Or was she walking into a trap?

When they came to a clearing she saw his

house, a small, modern structure nestled into a grove of pines.

"What a lovely house," she said as they walked up a flagstone walk. "And it's such a private setting."

"That's why I bought it," Mr. Tolchinsky said. He opened the front door. "Wait here in the vestibule. I'll call for the ambulance from my office."

Nancy stood in the entrance and peered around. Why was Mr. Tolchinsky so wary about letting people see his home? she wondered. What was he hiding?

He walked down a hallway to her left, opened a door, and went in. Nancy decided to take a quick look around while he was on the phone. She tiptoed into the living room, on her right.

The room was furnished sparingly. A low chrome and leather couch stood in front of a freestanding fireplace, the remains of a fire smoldering in the grate. A large window looked out onto an expanse of grass surrounded by pines.

The opposite wall was covered with framed photographs. Nancy went closer to see them.

In each picture stood the same man, young and dazzlingly handsome. In one, he stood with a former president of the United States. In another, with a Hollywood star. In yet another, he was shaking hands with a famous basketball player. And in each one, he was holding a book.

Nancy instantly recognized the dust jacket. The book had been one of her father's favorites. The man in the picture was none other than James Stanton, one of America's most famous writers.

Since her father had been one of his biggest fans, Nancy knew the story of James Stanton's life. His novels had been extraordinarily popular. A couple had even been made into movies. A decade ago Stanton stopped publishing his best-selling books. The word was he'd moved to a remote location and given up writing.

She remembered her father saying how odd it was that someone so talented and famous would give up like that and just disappear.

But what were all these pictures of James Stanton doing on Mr. Tolchinsky's wall? Nancy wondered.

She was so engrossed in her thoughts and the photographs that she didn't hear the footsteps behind her.

"How dare you invade my privacy!" Mr. Tolchinsky bellowed.

Nancy turned. When she saw Mr. Tolchinsky's face, she knew in an instant who he really was. His beard had been a good disguise.

"You're James Stanton, aren't you?" Nancy asked in amazement.

"Now you know my secret," he said grimly. "But can I trust you with it?" He took a step toward her.

11

A Faked Report

James Stanton stood with his hands on his hips and a fierce look on his face. "While I was calling an ambulance for your friend," he said, "you were betraying my trust by spying."

"That's not true," Nancy said. "I was simply looking at the pictures in full view on your wall."

"I suppose you have a point," he said stiffly. He put a hand to his beard and stroked it. "How did you know who I was?"

Nancy told him about her father and how he had been one of James Stanton's biggest admirers. "My father loves your books," she said. "Why did you stop writing?"

A frown passed over Mr. Stanton's face. "It was a personal decision," he said. Nancy could see he was struggling for the words. "I lost someone close to me. When she died, a part of me died as well. It's not that I *wanted* to stop writing. I *couldn't* write any longer."

Nancy saw the sadness in his face and knew Mr. Stanton was someone she could trust. He was telling the truth—at last.

"You didn't hurt those bats, did you?" she asked softly.

"I wouldn't harm a fly," Mr. Stanton said. "I only want to be left alone. You see, all this ruckus about the bats threatens my privacy. The last thing I want is a bunch of newspaper people running around here, poking their noses into everything. I've had enough of that."

"But the sooner it's resolved," Nancy said, "the sooner you'll have your peace and quiet."

"You have a point there," Mr. Stanton replied.

"So will you help me if I promise to keep your secret?" she asked.

"Help you with what?" he asked.

Nancy told him about the threats to Aunt Elizabeth, about Sarah and John Stryker and Ralph Bremer.

Mr. Stanton frowned. "I've seen Stryker and Bremer around here," he said. "I thought it had to do with the biological survey."

"It may and it may not," Nancy said. "I think something else may be going on as well."

"Such as?"

"I don't know," Nancy said. "But we need to

find out." She told Mr. Stanton about how the mystery car had followed them twice.

"But why are they after you?" he asked.

"Because I'm trying to get to the bottom of all this."

"Are you some kind of detective?" he asked.

Nancy laughed. "Yes, I am. I guess you could say I'm under cover, just like you."

Mr. Stanton graciously laughed at her joke. "Well, I'll help you if I can," he said.

In the distance, Nancy heard the wail of an ambulance. "I'd better be getting back to my friends," she said, heading for the door.

Mr. Stanton walked with her. "You'll keep my identity a secret?" he asked.

"I'll have to tell my friends," Nancy told him honestly. "I tell them everything, and they'll need to know that you're not under suspicion anymore."

Mr. Stanton frowned. "Well, swear them to secrecy," he said. "Do teenagers still do that?"

Nancy laughed. "Yes, we do," she assured him. "You can trust me."

He opened the door. "All right, Ms. Drew, you have my trust. Carry it safely."

"Please call me Nancy," she said. She put out her hand.

"And I'm James." He shook her hand, and

then Nancy hurried down the flagstone walk to the grove where her friends were waiting. What a story she had to tell them!

George rode with Bess in the ambulance to the hospital, while Nancy, Jessie, and Professor Noble followed in his car.

Several hours later Bess emerged from the emergency room on crutches. Her ankle was in a cast almost up to her knee.

"It's broken! Would you believe it? The doctor told me to rest as much as possible, and that's what I fully intend to do." She hobbled painfully toward the car. "I'll never learn to use these crutches," she said. Nancy and George helped her into the front seat of the car, and George put the crutches in back and settled herself around them.

"I hope that doesn't mean waiting on you hand and foot," George grumbled.

"You bet it does, dear cousin," Bess said. Everyone laughed.

Back at Aunt Elizabeth's, once they'd finished talking about Bess's injury, Nancy had the chance to tell everyone about James Stanton.

"Of course, you're all sworn to secrecy," she said when she had finished. "And I mean that," she said, giving Bess a long, hard look. If there was anything Bess loved, it was a juicy secret. "It's a good thing you can't get around," Nancy joked. "Maybe it will actually stay a secret."

Bess raised an eyebrow and grinned. "There's still the telephone. . . . Just kidding. His secret is safe with me."

"I knew that man was hiding something," Aunt Elizabeth said. "I thought it was something a little more scurrilous. Imagine, a world-famous writer in Fairport."

"Remember, now, you know nothing about this writer," Nancy reminded her.

"What writer?" Aunt Elizabeth retorted with a grin.

The next day at breakfast, Nancy announced it was time to pay a visit to the Town Hall.

"I think we need to talk to Mr. Stryker," she said. "He told us the town budget was exhausted from snow removal, and that it was a mild winter. He's met with Ralph Bremer, and they had an argument."

"That could mean anything," George said. "I'd like to know why he's been hanging around Mr. Stanton's . . . um, I mean, Mr. Tolchinsky's so much."

"You've got it," Nancy said brightly.

After assuring Bess they would tell her everything, absolutely everything, when they returned, Nancy and George headed into town.

Town Hall was just opening for the day. In the lobby, Nancy and George consulted a directory and located Mr. Stryker's office on the main floor and to the left.

When they arrived at his door, however, it was locked. Nancy poked her head into the doorway of the office next door. Ms. Oberdorf, the town secretary, was at her desk.

"I'm looking for Mr. Stryker," Nancy said. "Is he in?"

"Not right now," Ms. Oberdorf said. "He called a minute ago and said he'd be late."

"Do you know why?" Nancy asked.

Ms. Oberdorf shrugged. "He didn't say. And I didn't ask." She seemed a bit put out. "That means I've got to file all these papers myself." She shoved a stack of documents across her desk. "It's Chuck Danzig's habitat conservation plan and the dissenting opinions."

Her intercom rang, and she picked up the phone. After listening for a moment, she frowned. "No, I didn't know that. That's very odd. There was plenty of money in the road improvements fund the last time I looked." She paused. "All right," she said, and hung up. "Accounting," she said, getting up from her desk. "Seems to be a problem they think only I can fix." She stepped out into the hall. "Why don't you try later?" she said. "Mr. Stryker should be here after lunch."

Nancy watched Ms. Oberdorf go down the hall. When she knew she wouldn't be seen, she turned to the papers on the secretary's desk.

"Should we?" she asked George, nodding toward the papers.

"We didn't ask," George reminded her.

"No, we didn't," Nancy said. "But do we have to? These are public records. Look, there might be a clue in there. I can't pass this up."

Nancy stepped closer to the desk. "Keep watch," she told George, who stood outside glancing nervously down the hallway.

Nancy quickly leafed through the documents. There were a number of federal forms, dense with detail. There was also a transcript of the town meeting she'd attended and, finally, the habitat report from Chuck Danzig. Something in it caught her eye.

"What in the world—" Nancy exclaimed.

"Here she comes!" George whispered.

Nancy quickly restacked the papers and stepped out of the office to join George in the hall.

Ms. Oberdorf was looking down as she walked and didn't see Nancy and George until she got to the door of her office.

"Can I help you with anything else?" she asked. She was frowning.

"Did Chuck Danzig turn in his report yet?" Nancy asked.

"Mr. Stryker gave it to me yesterday to include in the package. He said it was the last thing that needed to be added. That's why I'm sending it all off today."

"That's good to hear," Nancy said.

"I'll be glad when this is over," Ms. Oberdorf said.

"I think we all will," Nancy said. She motioned to George. "Let's go."

When they reached the sidewalk, Nancy pulled George to one side. "Chuck's report said a cave had been found."

"What!" George exclaimed in disbelief. "How could Danzig know about a cave? He didn't even believe there was one at the town meeting. We're the only ones who know. The report's got to be a fake."

"Right," Nancy agreed exultantly. "But who gave Chuck's report to Ms. Oberdorf?"

"Mr. Stryker!" George answered. "Wow, this is getting exciting!"

Back at Aunt Elizabeth's, Nancy told Bess and George's aunt what they had discovered at the Town Hall.

"Mr. Stryker is involved in this somehow," Nancy insisted. "We've got to figure out how and why."

"Curiouser and curiouser," Aunt Elizabeth commented. The phone rang, and she rose to answer it in the hallway.

"It's for you," she said, motioning to Nancy. She covered the mouthpiece. "Mr. Tolchinsky," she said with a wink, and handed the receiver to Nancy.

Nancy took the phone and said hello.

"Nancy, it's James. Remember you asked for my help yesterday?"

"Yes," Nancy replied, wondering what was on his mind.

"Well, I think I've got another clue for you," he said.

"What is it?" Nancy asked eagerly.

"I'm not really sure," James said. "Something I've found in the woods."

"Can you tell me what it is?" Nancy begged.

"I could if I knew what it was," James replied. "How soon can you get here?"

"Sooner than you think," Nancy replied. She hung up the phone, grabbed George's hand, and pulled her out the door. "We'll be back!" she called.

"What's going on?" George asked as they jumped into the car.

"I have no idea," Nancy said, backing out of the driveway. "James Stanton has found something he thinks we should see."

It didn't take long to reach James's house. Since the driveway was almost hidden from the road, Nancy slowed down as she searched for it.

She saw movement in the woods. Several yards away, Sarah was about to hop onto her bike.

Nancy saw that Sarah recognized her behind the wheel. The girl pedaled away quickly.

What was Sarah doing here? Nancy wondered. And did it have anything to do with what James had found in the woods?

12

There . . . and Gone!

James Stanton was waiting for them at the door to his house.

"We just saw Sarah Connor biking away," Nancy told him when he joined them on the flagstone walk. "She looked guilty."

James thought for a moment. "Is that the girl whose brother was killed?"

Nancy nodded.

"I've seen her around here a number of times," James said. "She always looks guilty to me, too. But I just thought she was doing some kind of teenage thing. Teenagers often look guilty to me, I guess because lots of times they're doing things they shouldn't be.

"Now, wait a minute," George said.

"Present company excluded, of course," James said, grinning. "Now come on, let me show you what I've found. It's in the stream."

As they set off into the woods, he said, "I just don't know what it is." He pushed past some brush, and they were on the banks of the stream.

In the middle of the stream, held up by some wooden crossbars, was a coarsely made wooden structure several yards long and higher at one end than the other. It was shaped like a box, without the top lid, and lined with wire mesh.

"Any idea what that is?" James asked Nancy and George.

Nancy shook her head. She'd never seen anything like it before. It looked like an antique, except when she got closer she saw that the wood was new and still smelled of pine.

"Do you think your professor friend might know what it is?" James asked.

"That's a great idea," Nancy said. She turned to George. "Do you know where the college is? We could go over there and ask him."

"My great-uncle was a professor there," George responded. "We used to go for picnics on the grounds when we visited in the summer. I think I can find the way."

They walked back to James's house.

"Call me and let me know what you find out," he said when they reached the car.

Nancy promised to call, and she and George hopped into the car.

On the way, George took a couple of wrong

turns, but before long they drove through a gate in the brick walls of Fairport College. They parked in front of the main building and went in. A directory on the wall told them Professor Noble's office was on the second floor.

"I hope he's in," Nancy said.

He was, sitting at his desk, writing. When he saw Nancy and George, he hopped up.

"I was just finishing the report for the fish and wildlife proposal that states we've found the cave," he said. "Would you like to take a look at it?" He handed it to Nancy.

"You're not going to believe this," she said, "but I discovered this morning that Chuck's report mentioned it was found."

"What!" Professor Noble exclaimed. "We only found it yesterday. And Chuck said it didn't exist. He didn't even want to join me in looking for it."

"I know," Nancy said. "Ms. Oberdorf said Mr. Stryker gave Chuck's report to her yesterday."

"Why would Chuck give John the report, anyway?" Professor Noble asked, perplexed.

"I don't think he did," Nancy said. "I think Mr. Stryker did something fishy with it. But that's not why we're here." She went on to tell him what they'd seen in the stream near James's house.

"Could you draw a picture for me?" Professor Noble asked. "That might help."

Nancy quickly drew a rough sketch on the scrap of paper he handed to her.

Professor Noble wrinkled his brow as he looked at it. "The last time I saw something like that was in a book about the Gold Rush. It's a sluice. People use it to separate gold from pebbles in stream beds."

"But we're not in California," George said. "Who would look for gold here?"

"There've always been rumors that there's gold in that stream," Professor Noble said. "It's called the shining stream."

"The shining stream . . ." Nancy murmured.

"What?" Professor Noble said.

"The shining stream," Nancy said with mounting excitment. "I heard Mr. Stryker mention it at the coffee shop."

"That's right!" George exclaimed.

"The rumor is that there's a mother lode at the end of it, so rich it would make whoever found it a millionaire," Professor Noble said. "It's highly unlikely there's gold there, but you know how rumors are. Someone might just be having some fun with it.

"But from what you've described," he went on, "it looks as though they've sunk some money into their operation. I'd say they think they're onto something. Of course, they'd have to have a permit to do that kind of sluicing."

119

"A permit from the town?" Nancy asked.

Professor Noble nodded. "That kind of sluicing can pollute the waters downstream. They'd have to show they have additional equipment to take care of it."

"Then we need to return to the Town Hall," Nancy said, "to see if anyone's filed a permit."

George cleared her throat. "Nancy, isn't this kind of a wild-goose chase? What we really need to find out is who's threatening Aunt E. and who killed the bats."

"I know," Nancy agreed. "But I have a hunch this is all tied together. Someone is looking for gold in that stream. And my hunch is it's Mr. Stryker. And maybe Mr. Bremer, too."

Professor Noble thought for a moment. "Do you expect to find a permit?" he finally asked.

Nancy shook her head. "No. If those two are looking for gold, they'd want to keep it a secret, wouldn't they?"

Martin and George nodded.

"Then let's find out for sure," Nancy replied. "Maybe this is the missing piece to this mystery we've been looking for!"

A quick search through the permits on file at the Town Hall turned up nothing, just as Nancy suspected. They were about to leave the Permit Office when Mr. Stryker came in.

"What brings you to Town Hall?" he asked them pleasantly.

"Just a friendly visit," Nancy said.

"Well, I hope you're enjoying your stay in Fairport," he said, and walked away.

When they were back outside, George turned to her friend. "That was close," she said.

"I hope we didn't tip him off to what we're up to," Nancy said with a worried frown. "We need to go back to James's. I want to take another look at that equipment. Maybe we'll find some clues that will lead us to Mr. Stryker and Mr. Bremer."

"Could we have some lunch first?" George begged. "I'm starving."

The coffee shop was almost empty because it was way past lunchtime. Nancy and George ordered. While they waited for their food, Nancy laid out the clues.

"We have someone who's been threatening Aunt Elizabeth," she said. "It could be Sarah. Or it could be someone else."

"And we have someone who's killed the bats," George said.

"And someone who's looking for gold in the shining stream," Nancy went on.

"And someone who changed Chuck's report," George reminded her.

"The question is," Nancy said, picking up the hamburger the waitress had set before her, "are

121

these things part of a bigger thing or are they completely unrelated?"

"What's your guess?" George asked, biting into a ham sandwich.

"My guess is there's one more clue we need to have this all make sense," Nancy said. "And we've got to find it fast."

After Nancy told James Stanton what they'd learned from Professor Noble, he was more than willing to give them permission to revisit the stream. Remembering some of the landmarks along the way, Nancy soon led them to the edge of the woods, where the stream meandered.

"What in the world?" she exclaimed.

"It's gone!" George cried.

The stream was empty. It was as if the sluice had never existed.

"Someone must have moved it," Nancy said. "They must know we found it."

"But how could they know?" George demanded. "We've told no one."

"But we did run into Mr. Stryker," Nancy reminded her. "And it would have been easy for him to ask the people at the Permit Office what we were doing there. Obviously, he's onto us now or the equipment would still be here."

"That makes sense," George said. "What do we do next?"

"Let's go back to Aunt E.'s," Nancy said, "and put all our heads together."

They walked back to the car. They were just about to get in when Nancy saw a young figure on a bicycle quickly pedaling out into the road.

"It's Sarah!" she exclaimed, and ran after her. "Wait!" she called.

When Sarah saw Nancy chasing her, she pedaled faster, glancing behind her to make sure Nancy wasn't catching up.

A car came speeding around the curve. "Sarah! Stop!" Nancy called. "Watch out!" Sarah's bike wobbled as she struggled to regain her balance. The car sped toward her.

"Oh, George!" Nancy cried. "I can't look!"

13

A Crack in the Puzzle

"She's okay," George said, grabbing Nancy's arm. Sarah had swerved her bicycle to the side seconds before the car would have hit her. The car traveled on for several yards, then stopped.

Sarah was standing by the side of the road, her sides heaving as she tried to catch her breath. Nancy and George ran up to her.

"You could have been hurt!" Nancy cried. "Are you all right?"

"Just scared," Sarah said.

The driver of the car was standing in the middle of the road looking at them.

"You could have been killed!" he yelled. "Watch where you're going."

"I'm sorry," Sarah said, hanging her head.

"Be more careful next time," he told her as he walked back to his car. "You know, a boy was killed here not so long ago. This road needs to be wider." He climbed into his car and drove off.

"And you need to drive slower," George said under her breath.

Nancy took Sarah's bike and steered it onto James's property. Sarah sat down on a boulder and put her face in her hands.

"Why did you run away from me?" Nancy asked.

"Because I don't trust you. Because you're against me," Sarah said. "Because you suspect me of things I haven't done!"

Nancy sat down next to her. Out of the corner of her eye she saw George approach, but she waved her away. George sauntered back to their car.

"I'll trust you if you tell me the truth," Nancy said. "But you haven't been honest with me. We've discovered the cave where the bats hibernate, and all the bats have been killed."

Sarah looked up at Nancy, shocked. "They're dead? Who would do such a thing?"

"We have some suspects," Nancy said.

"And I'm one of them, aren't I?" Sarah asked. She jumped to her feet.

"Well, you certainly don't like bats," Nancy reminded her. "And like the driver of that car, you're for widening the road. Killing the bats would eliminate the obstacle to the widening, wouldn't it?''

"I wouldn't harm the bats," Sarah said.

"Then why are you here?" Nancy asked. "This is the second time I've seen you in this spot in the past couple of days."

Sarah put her head down and then looked Nancy straight in the eye. "My brother died at this corner. I come to mourn him. Sometimes I leave flowers at the spot where he died. That's why I come here."

Nancy put an arm around Sarah's shoulder, expecting her to shrug it off, but she didn't. "I want to trust you. I really do. But you know I've got to find out who's threatening Mrs. Porter, and so I have to suspect anyone who seems likely. It was your car that tried to push me off the road."

"But I swear to you that it wasn't me!" Sarah exclaimed. "And I have proof."

"You do?" Nancy asked.

Sarah reached into her backpack. "After you left that night, I searched my car. I knew someone had to have taken it out of my driveway." She took out a pad of paper and handed it to Nancy. "This is what I found."

Nancy took the pad from Sarah. It was a receipt pad, the kind that made duplicates with carbon paper. When she saw the name of the store on it, she caught her breath: Fairport Hardware.

"Why didn't you show this to us sooner?" Nancy asked. "Or to the police?"

"Because I didn't know who to trust," Sarah said. "I knew someone was out to frame me for something I hadn't done. Can you blame me?"

Nancy turned the pad over in her hand, mulling over the implications. "No, I can't," she admitted. "I'm glad you told me."

"What does this mean?" Sarah asked her.

"Why don't you come with me?" Nancy said, and pulled Sarah to her feet. "We have a lot to talk about."

Back at Aunt Elizabeth's, Nancy, George, Bess, and Sarah gathered in the parlor. It was time to begin to put the pieces of the puzzle together.

"We suspect that John Stryker and Ralph Bremer are looking for gold in the brook," Nancy said. "I overheard them talking about a shining stream at the coffee shop the other day."

"And we know that Mr. Stryker changed Chuck's report, saying the cave existed even before we found it," she went on.

"Why would he do that?" Sarah asked.

"I suspect because he doesn't want the widening equipment on that road. The workers would be going into the woods or be out on the road for months," Nancy explained. "He couldn't look for gold in secret with all that activity going on nearby. And he was doing it in secret. He never filed a permit."

"So is that why he was so agreeable about the bats?" Aunt Elizabeth asked. "Not because he had any sympathy for the conservationists but because widening the road threatened his own interests?"

"That's right," Nancy said. "At least, that's what I think."

"But what I don't understand is why someone as smart as Mr. Stryker would get taken in like that by a rumor of gold," Bess said. "He's the town manager, after all."

"I think Ralph Bremer must play a role in motivating him," George suggested. "After all, his hardware store isn't doing so well."

"That's a good point," Nancy said.

"But who killed the bats? And why?" Bess asked. "And who's been threatening Aunt Elizabeth?"

"And why?" George echoed.

"That's what we're going to find out," Nancy resolved. "We're going back to the Town Hall right now to ask Mr. Stryker. And I hope he gives us a straight answer."

* * *

It was late in the afternoon by the time they arrived at Town Hall. Nancy, George, and Sarah marched into Mr. Stryker's office and found him at his desk.

"Well," he said, looking up, "if it isn't the young detective and her friends."

"How do you know I'm a detective?" Nancy asked.

"Word gets around in a small town," Mr. Stryker said.

"Mr. Stryker," Nancy said in a no-nonsense tone of voice, "I have reason to believe that you've been looking for gold on town property not far from Hank Tolchinsky's house. Is that true?"

Mr. Stryker laughed. "Looking for gold? You must be kidding."

"No, I'm not," Nancy said. "And I also know you forged Chuck Danzig's report for the Fish and Wildlife Service. Chuck never found the cave, but we did. We found it yesterday—filled with dead bats."

Mr. Stryker rose from his desk. "I refuse to discuss this with you," he declared. "If I answer any questions, they'll be from an officer of the law. And believe me, if you approach the Fairport police and tell them your suspicions, they'll laugh in your face!"

"Well, we'll see about that, won't we," Nancy said. She turned and began to leave, followed by George and Sarah.

"Are you going to the police?" Mr. Stryker called after her.

Nancy turned to face him. "Does that worry you?" she retorted.

"Me?" Mr. Stryker laughed. "I don't have a worry in the world."

"What are you going to do?" Sarah asked when they'd left the Town Hall. "Are you going to the police?"

"I think it's time," Nancy said. "We have evidence now with that receipt pad you found in your car. And we also know he's changed an official report. Chuck Danzig will testify that he never mentioned that the cave was found. I don't have any authority over Mr. Stryker, but the police do."

The police station was just around the corner. Nancy was glad to see that Officer Spinetti was on duty. She listened carefully while Nancy told her the whole story.

"It certainly sounds as if you have evidence on both Stryker and Bremer," she said. "I have to tell you, though, that I'm shocked. John Stryker has always been, in my experience, completely

130

honest and straightforward. What could be making him behave this way?"

"I'm not sure," Nancy said. "But what are we going to do about it?"

"I don't know if I can help you," Officer Spinetti said, "much as I'd like to. Why don't you young ladies head back home? We can talk about it in the morning if you're still suspicious."

"Why wouldn't she help us?" George asked after they'd left the police station.

"She's loyal to her townspeople, I guess," Nancy said. "She probably thinks we're just a bunch of out-of-town teenagers with overactive imaginations."

On the way back to Aunt Elizabeth's, Nancy had a chance to mull over the mystery. Everything certainly was pointing to Mr. Stryker as the source of most of the trouble. But she couldn't figure out what motive he had for threatening Aunt Elizabeth.

After dropping Sarah off at her house and promising to bring her bicycle back the next day, they drove to Aunt Elizabeth's.

George was pulling the car into the driveway when Nancy noticed that even though it was dusk, the lights were off in the house.

"Curious," Nancy murmured. She and George got out of the car.

When they arrived at the front door, Nancy

noticed that it was open. A chill went down her spine. Something didn't feel right.

When she pushed the door open farther and switched on the light, she realized why.

There, tied to a chair with a gag across her mouth, was Bess.

14

Aunt Elizabeth Disappears

Bess's eyes were terrified as Nancy untied the gag.

"Where's Aunt E.?" George asked anxiously.

Bess started to cry. "She's gone!" she exclaimed. "I've never been so frightened in my life!" Nancy undid the ropes and helped Bess stand up and hobble over to the sofa. Bess sank down, and Nancy lifted her legs onto the sofa and plumped up a pillow behind her head.

"Aunt E. is gone?" George cried. "Where?"

Bess shook her head. "I don't know. Some man took her away."

"A man!" George exclaimed. "Bess, tell us what happened!"

Bess wiped her eyes. "I was keeping Aunt Elizabeth company in the kitchen while she made dinner," Bess said. She started crying again.

"Bess, I know this has been awful for you, but you have to tell us what happened," Nancy said gently to her friend. "Aunt Elizabeth's life may be in danger."

"I know," Bess said, wiping her eyes with the back of her hand. "That's why I'm so upset."

"So, Aunt Elizabeth was making dinner," George prompted her. "Then what?"

"This man appeared in the doorway," Bess said. "He was dressed all in black, and he had a ski mask on so we couldn't see who he was. He pointed a gun at Aunt Elizabeth. I think she thought he was a burglar."

"What did he do?" Nancy asked, urging Bess along.

"He told me to get up and go into the hall-way," Bess said. "I told him I had a broken ankle, but he didn't care. He told me to sit down, and then he tied and gagged me."

"Could you recognize his voice?" Nancy asked.

Again, Bess shook her head. "He was trying to disguise it, I could tell."

"Did he take Aunt Elizabeth with him?" George asked. Bess was beginning to shake— Nancy could see—imagining her aunt's peril.

"Yes," Bess said. "He said he was taking her away, and I'd better not try to find her or the same thing would happen to me."

Nancy looked at George. Could it have been Mr. Stryker?

"Bess, do you think someone else might have been waiting for him outside?" Nancy asked.

Bess shook her head. "He left the front door open. I could see the car was empty."

George patted Bess's shoulder. "Are you okay?" she asked. "How's the ankle?"

"I guess it's okay," Bess said, "but I'm still scared."

"We all are," Nancy said. She looked at George.

"What are you thinking?" George asked.

"That it had to be Mr. Stryker," Nancy said. "But since he didn't have his sidekick with him, I think we'd better track him down."

"You mean Mr. Bremer?" Bess asked.

"Yes," Nancy replied. "Let's check his store. He may know all about this. Or he may not. He and Stryker haven't exactly seemed the best of friends lately. Maybe they've had a falling-out, and he'll be willing to tell us everything he knows. If he understands the trouble he's in, he should be willing to."

"Let's go then," George said.

She and Nancy helped Bess into the car. They knew Bess wouldn't want to stay in the house by herself. And Nancy didn't know how safe she'd be if she did.

Most of the stores on the green were closed by the time they arrived there. They couldn't believe their luck when they saw that Fairport Hardware was still open. Mr. Bremer was behind the cash register.

Bess stayed behind in the car, and Nancy and George went into the store.

"Hello," Nancy said, making her voice much more friendly sounding then she actually felt.

"Evening," he said.

"Are you about to close?" Nancy asked.

"Not if you want something," Mr. Bremer replied.

"Tell me, if I wanted to find gold in a stream, what would I need?" she asked. "I figure that I could probably find the right tools here, in a hardware store."

An uneasy look passed over his face. "I'm sorry," he said, coming out from behind the cash register. "But I'm about to close for the night. Could you come back tomorrow?"

He was going to be tough, Nancy could tell.

"Not until you tell me what you and John Stryker have been up to out in the woods near Hank Tolchinsky's place," she said calmly.

"I don't know what you're talking about," Mr. Bremer said.

"Yes, you do," Nancy insisted firmly. "And you'd better tell us what you know, because I think your friend has just done something that's going to get him into a lot of trouble."

Mr. Bremer looked stricken. "What do you mean?"

"I mean it looks as if he's kidnapped Elizabeth Porter," Nancy told him bluntly. "If I were you, I'd tell me everything, or you'll be charged as an accomplice."

"I know nothing about this!" Mr. Bremer shouted.

"Well, what do you know about this?" Nancy asked, pulling the receipt pad Sarah had given her out of her jeans pocket and slapping it on the counter. "It was found in Sarah Connor's car the night it pushed my car off the road. You dropped it there, didn't you?"

"Stryker made me take her car!" Mr. Bremer yelled. "I tell you, the man's crazy."

"Why not tell us what you know?" Nancy asked again. "We'll find out anyway. If you cooperate, maybe the police will go easier on you in the end."

Mr. Bremer walked over to a stool and sat down wearily.

"You don't know how bad it's been," he began with a sigh. "My business has been failing for the past year, and I've been hard pressed for money. So I approached Stryker with a deal. There've always been rumors about gold in that stream

137

near Tolchinsky's, and I told Stryker if he bank-rolled a sluicing operation, I'd split the profits when we found the mother lode."

"And he agreed?" Nancy asked. At last he was talking.

Mr. Bremer nodded. "He said he was having his own money troubles. He loved to sail, and he'd sunk a lot of money into a boat and needed more money to enter races. So we went in on it together."

"And then the road controversy hit?" Nancy asked. It was a logical question.

"Right. We'd just begun to find some gold, although not enough to keep Stryker happy. But he went ballistic over this bat thing. He knew if the town decided to widen the road, our operation was doomed."

"Is he the one who was threatening my aunt?" George asked.

"Yes." Mr. Bremer gave a nasty laugh. "He said he knew Mrs. Porter well and that if she got her back up about something, she'd be unstoppable. So he egged her on with those threats—the phone calls, the stuffed bat, causing the car accidents. It was all done to make her even more resolute."

Ah! At last, Nancy understood Stryker's motive. It was a fiendishly clever use of reverse psychology. And he must have thought that killing the bats would be the best possible way to get Elizabeth working for his evil purpose.

"So you ran us off the road," Nancy said. "But how did you know my car?"

"I saw you getting into it in front of my store one day," Mr. Bremer admitted.

"And the bats that were killed. Did you two do that?"

At this point, Mr. Bremer looked genuinely surprised. "No, it wasn't me. I started to distance myself from Stryker after we ran you off the road. I figured I'd shut down the sluicing operation and try to find my money some other way, rather than do what Stryker wanted."

Nancy believed him. He looked tired. Tired and relieved to have confessed.

"Do you have any idea where he could have taken Mrs. Porter?" Nancy asked. "It looks as if he must be the one who kidnapped her."

Mr. Bremer thought for a moment. "Stryker has a cabin, a shack really, out in the woods not far from Tolchinsky's house," he said. "That's the only place I can think of."

"Tell us how to get there," Nancy said.

Mr. Bremer quickly gave them directions and even drew a rough map on the back of a piece of paper.

"Look, if we go, will you try to get to him first?" Nancy asked him. She wasn't ready to trust him completely, after all.

Mr. Bremer shook his head. "I'm done with that man," he said.

Nancy turned to George. "Let's go then. This is our best chance."

Nancy thanked Mr. Bremer and opened the door to leave.

Mr. Bremer called after her, "If I were you, I'd get the police to come along. You don't know what that man is capable of."

Nancy, Bess, and George huddled together in the car. "Should we get the police?" Nancy asked. "Officer Spinetti wasn't too helpful before."

"But now that Aunt E.'s been kidnapped, she will be!" George exclaimed. "Let's go."

Of course, when Officer Spinetti heard that Aunt Elizabeth had been kidnapped, she immediately agreed to help Nancy and her friends.

"Do you still think Mr. Stryker is behind all this?" she asked Nancy.

Nancy nodded. "I'm convinced."

Officer Spinetti sighed. "All right, then. We'll do this right." Before she left the station, she put out an all-points bulletin for Mr. Stryker's car.

It was dark as Officer Spinetti drove carefully along Old Fairport Road, following the directions

Mr. Bremer had given Nancy. At a fork in the road, she turned off and soon came to another fork. A dirt road led into the woods. Soon a cabin appeared in the headlights.

Nancy hopped out. Officer Spinetti got out and motioned for her to stay near the car. "Police," she said, and knocked on the door of the cabin. When she got no answer, she pushed on the door. Nancy crept behind her. The door swung open easily. In the moonlight streaming through the windows Nancy could see that it was empty.

Dejected, she returned to the police car with Officer Spinetti.

"You won't believe this," George said when they got in. "But according to the radio, Stryker's car's just been spotted."

"Where?" Nancy asked.

"On Old Fairport Road," Bess said with excitement. "Right on that curve near Hank Tolchinsky's place. Let's go!"

15

Rescue in the Dark

Officer Spinetti's car tore down the road with Nancy, Bess, and George in the backseat.

"Why would he be there?" George asked.

"I have a sneaking suspicion it has to do with the stream," Nancy said. Then a thought burst into her head. "Oh no," she whispered.

"What?" George asked.

"I may be crazy, but I think he's taken Aunt Elizabeth to the cave!"

"Aunt E. in the cave!" George cried. "This is just awful."

"What I don't understand is what he thinks he's going to gain by doing it," Nancy went on.

"He's desperate," George replied in a low, tight voice. "Remember what Mr. Bremer said?"

Officer Spinetti's car squealed to a stop. She hopped out, followed by Nancy and George. Bess stayed inside the police car.

142

A car was parked by the side of the road. It had to be Mr. Stryker's. But it was empty.

"The cave," Nancy said.

Officer Spinetti sucked in her breath. "Oh boy," was all she said.

"I think we could find our way there in the dark," Nancy said. "Do you have a flashlight?"

Officer Spinetti took a high-intensity flashlight off her belt. "Lead on," she said to Nancy. "If that man has hurt so much as a hair on Mrs. Porter's head, I'll personally throw him in a jail cell and lock it with pleasure!"

As quickly as they could, the girls and the police officer walked through the inky blackness. It was hard to get her bearings, Nancy discovered, with only what the flashlight could pick out in the woods. But soon enough they reached the clearing. Then it was easy, using the stream as a guide, to find their way to the site of the cave.

When they got there, they could see that the opening of the cave, which had once been so carefully covered, was now in disarray, as if someone had been pawing through the camouflage.

George ran to the opening. "Aunt E.! Aunt E.!" she called down the hole.

"George?" a weak voice answered from within.

"She's in there! You were right!" George cried, hugging Nancy.

"Are you okay?" Officer Spinetti called into the hole.

"I'm fine, but it's dark down here!" Aunt Elizabeth called back. "And it doesn't smell too good, either."

"I'm going to reach down with my hand," Officer Spinetti said, falling to her knees in front of the hole. "I'll shine the flashlight down. Can you see my hand?"

"Yes," Aunt Elizabeth said.

"Then grab it," Officer Spinetti ordered. "I'll pull you out." She turned to Nancy and George. "I may need some help."

The girls kneeled next to Officer Spinetti and helped pull Aunt Elizabeth out.

When she was back aboveground, Aunt Elizabeth sat calmly at the edge of the opening. "Well, that was an experience!" she said.

"That's the understatement of the day," Nancy said.

George threw her arms around her aunt and exclaimed, "Thank goodness you're safe!"

"But where's Mr. Stryker?" Nancy asked. "Did he leave you here alone?"

Aunt Elizabeth nodded. "The man's gone mad. I kept asking him what he thought he was trying to prove, and he kept telling me . . . well, nothing."

"Where could he have gone?" George wondered.

"I don't know," Aunt Elizabeth said. "All I know is that he brought me here, pushed me down into the cave, and then took off."

"Come on," Officer Spinetti said, offering Aunt Elizabeth an arm to lean on as she rose. "You've had enough excitement for one night."

They returned through the woods to the road.

"Look!" Nancy cried, pointing.

Mr. Stryker's car was gone.

Officer Spinetti's police radio crackled. She ducked into her car to hear the message.

"He's been spotted again," she said. "His car's in front of the Town Hall."

"What in the world?" Aunt Elizabeth moaned.

Nancy and George got in the back, and Aunt Elizabeth sat next to Officer Spinetti.

"Are you all right?" Bess asked Aunt Elizabeth. "I was so worried about you."

"I'm fine, Bess. I'm glad to see you're all right, too. What a brute!"

Officer Spinetti took the curves carefully and skillfully.

"Why is the jerk at Town Hall?" George asked. "That's the first place we'd think to look for him."

145

"I think this is more complicated than we thought," Nancy said. "Remember, Mr. Bremer said he was desperate for money."

"That's why he was looking for gold."

"Right. But it wasn't working out."

"Not exactly," George said. "At least, not as much as he needed."

"Do you remember when we were at Town Hall and Mrs. Oberdorf got called into the accounting department?" Nancy asked.

George nodded. "That's when you looked at those papers on Mr. Stryker's desk."

"We heard her say money was missing from the road improvement fund and she had to find out where it had gone," Nancy said.

"I remember. But what are you suggesting?" George asked.

"Remember on the day we arrived how Mr. Stryker said there wasn't any money to widen the road? That the snowfalls last year had wiped out the budget?"

"Yes," George replied, still mystified.

"Well, I caught a glimpse of the local newspaper the other day, and there was an article about how mild the winter had been last year."

"That doesn't fit in with what he said, does it?" George replied.

"No, it doesn't. And I get the feeling that the

lack of funds in the budget is the result of Mr. Stryker's tinkering with them. Remember how Mr. Bremer said he needed money to race his boat? I think he's probably embezzled funds. That's another reason why he wouldn't want the road widened. If the town wanted the money to pay for it, he'd be found out."

"Nancy, you're a genius!" George exclaimed. They pulled up in front of the Town Hall.

"We'll see," Nancy responded dryly. "Let's hope we can get this settled tonight."

Officer Spinetti hopped out of the car, with Nancy and George right behind her. She tried the front door.

"It's locked," she said. "I can get a key back at the station." As they turned away, Mr. Stryker pushed the door open from the inside, ready to step out. When he saw the women on the sidewalk, he bolted back into the building.

"Catch him!" George cried. She grabbed the door so it wouldn't slam shut.

Nancy darted through the door. She was fast enough to catch up to Mr. Stryker. She grabbed him by the waist and butted her knees against the backs of his legs to bring him to his knees.

"Nice work," Officer Spinetti said, running up to them. "What do you say we go over to the police station?" she said to Mr. Stryker, who lay on the floor in a crumpled heap. "I'm a pretty good listener, and you've got a lot of talking to do."

Several days later, Nancy, George, and Bess, having packed their bags, were sitting in Aunt Elizabeth's kitchen. She was going to drive them to the train station. The rental car had been returned the day before, and it was time to go back to River Heights.

Aunt Elizabeth was in the vestibule, about to put on her jacket, when the doorbell rang. "Why, hello!" Nancy heard Aunt Elizabeth say. "How nice of you to come."

Aunt Elizabeth came into the kitchen with a sheepish-looking Sarah behind her. Sarah was carrying a gift box, which she handed to Nancy.

"This is for you," she said, looking down. "With thanks."

"Oh, Sarah," Nancy said, touched by her kind gesture. "You didn't have to buy me a present."

"Open it," Sarah said with a shy smile. "When you see what it is, you'll know why."

Nancy opened the package. Nestled within some crisp tissue paper was a stuffed bat exactly like the one they had found hanging from the rafters of Aunt Elizabeth's porch.

Nancy laughed and held it up for all to see.

"Now that Mr. Stryker's locked up," Sarah

said, "you don't have to worry about him stealing yours the way he stole mine."

Nancy laughed. "It's amazing what he did to cast suspicion on you. Stealing the bat, stealing your car . . ." She shook her head. "And those phone calls. I guess you have to give him credit for having a fiendish mind."

"Well, the town owes you its congratulations," Sarah said. "After that article in the *Fairport News* yesterday about the real story behind the road widening, everyone's been talking. Now we know it was Mr. Stryker that was causing the problem. Imagine, embezzling all that money!"

"It was quite a shock," Aunt Elizabeth said.

"The way he turned us against one another," Sarah said to Aunt Elizabeth, "when he knew that if he hadn't embezzled, the town would have had enough money to solve the problem."

"Oh?" Aunt Elizabeth said, surprised. "Do you have a solution to the road widening versus the bats controversy?"

"Yes," Sarah said. "I think I do." She smiled broadly. It was the first time Nancy had seen Sarah smile in that way.

"Then tell us," Bess encouraged her. "I like happy endings."

"Well, we were so caught up in our separate points of view that we never got to the point where we could think of compromises," Sarah said. "And there's a simple way to make everybody happy—both the people who want the road widened, like me, and the people who want to save the bats, like Mrs. Porter."

"I knew there had to be a compromise somewhere," Aunt Elizabeth proclaimed.

"And there is. I'm going to propose at next week's town meeting that we widen the road."

"That takes care of your part," Aunt Elizabeth said. "What about mine?"

"Right," Sarah said brightly. "We won't widen where the grove of oaks is. I know that part of the road well, and wc can solve the whole problem by building a bike path through the grove. It would cost a little more"—she took a deep breath—"but it would save the bats."

"Sarah, that's wonderful!" Aunt Elizabeth cried and threw her arms around her.

"It *is* wonderful," Nancy said. "Good for you, Sarah. I'm sure everyone will think it's a great idea."

"If they're still willing to listen to me," Sarah said apologetically. "I was a little strident, you know."

"But all for a good cause, wouldn't you say?" Aunt Elizabeth asked.

Talking and laughing, they agreed.

"And now, it's time to go, or we'll miss your

train," Aunt Elizabeth reminded George, Nancy, and Bess. "Sarah, would you like to come along?"

"I'd love to," she said. "Is there room in the car?"

"Of course," Aunt Elizabeth replied. "Always."

As Mrs. Porter was closing the door, a car pulled up, and Professor Noble and Jessie hopped out.

"I'm glad we made it in time," Professor Noble said. "We couldn't let you leave without a proper Fairport send-off." He reached back into the car and handed Nancy, Bess, and George each bouquets of yellow daffodils.

"They're lovely," Nancy said. "Thank you."

The group stood outside in the warm spring sun, sharing their memories of the past week. When Sarah told Jessie and Professor Noble her plan, they cheered with relief.

"We couldn't have reached this compromise without you," Professor Noble said to Nancy. "We all appreciate what you've done."

"Thanks," Nancy said. "But all of us deserve credit. I couldn't have done it alone."

"And now it's back to River Heights," Bess said. "But before I go, will you all sign my cast? What a story I have to go along with it!"

R.L. STINE'S
GHOSTS OF FEAR STREET®